AT WOLFE'S DOOR
The Nero Wolfe Novels of
REX STOUT

At Wolfe's Door
THE NERO WOLFE NOVELS OF
REX STOUT

by

J. Kenneth Van Dover

JAMES A. ROCK & COMPANY, PUBLISHERS
ROCKVILLE • MARYLAND

Address comments and inquiries to:

JAMES A. ROCK & COMPANY, PUBLISHERS
9710 Traville Gateway Drive, Box 305
Rockville, MD 20850

E-mail:
jrock@rockpublishing.com   lrock@senseofwonderpress.com
Internet URL: www.RockPublishing.com

Paperbound ISBN: 0-918736-52-8
Hardbound ISBN: 0-918736-51-x

Printed in the United States of America

CONTENTS

Preface to
the Second Edition

Unlike old generals, some old detective story writers refuse even to fade away. The Victorian world of Sherlock Holmes, the interwar world of Hercule Poirot, even the tough, Prohibition and Depression world of Sam Spade and Philip Marlowe have evidently retained their appeal into the twentieth century. Detective novels are, in their nature, tied to their times—the details which the detective distinguishes himself by noticing are inherently of a particular historical moment, but some are evidently well-conceived and well-executed enough to last well beyond their moment. Rex Stout's Nero Wolfe novels evidently belong to this class.

A quarter century after his death, the Nero Wolfe books remain in print (on, it is reported, "a rotating basis") and, as a result of a very popular A & E television series which premiered in 2000, their continuing presence seems assured. The cadre of enthusiasts who comprise the Wolfe Pack and publish *The Gazette* still prosper (their website is www.nerowolfe.org). A number of other Wolfean websites have appeared on the internet. It is this continuing interest which, I hope, justifies this new edition of *At Wolfe's Door*.

The success of the series is significant especially because the scripts remained remarkably faithful to the novels. The programs are set in the period, and much of the dialogue is lifted directly from the novel. Effective novelistic dialogue is not usually effective screen dialogue, as Raymond Chandler discovered when he worked on the script for the 1944 film of James M. Cain's *Double Indemnity*. The A & E series was able to adopt verbatim both the sharp exchanges between Wolfe and Archie, and as well Archie's narration in voiceover. Credit certainly goes to the skills of the repertory actors who played the roles, and especially to Maury Chaykin and Timothy Hutton; but it was Stout who supplied the language and the characters who speak it. And it was Stout who created in words the real pleasures of the novels: the voices and ideas, the rooms and the routines. Producer Michael Jaffe realized this, and with great care recreated those pleasures on film.

And it is clearly the characters and the language which they use that sustain the series. The television series confirms what was evident in the novels: although Stout chose the discipline of the most plot-driven form of a plot-driven genre, plot was not his forte. He constructs his narratives as a sequence of encounters, more in the manner of the Hard-boiled detective story than of the Classical, with its baroque entanglements which often require diagrams and tables to clarify what must have happened. As a result, they are well-suited for adaptation to film. But where the Hard-boiled encounters are violent confrontations, usually ending in fisticuffs and gunplay, Wolfe's confrontations (with Archie as well as with clients, witnesses, and law enforcement officers) are verbal, and elegant without being precious (in the vein of Philo Vance, Charlie Chan, or Ellery Queen). And this verbal elegance in a succession of confrontations works on video as well as the noir versions of the more physical and deadly confrontations of the Hard-boiled worked on film.

I have made minor corrections in the body of *At Wolfe's Door*. Credit for many of these can be assigned to Bettina Silber, a sharp reader of Wolfe, as well as of *At Wolfe's Door*. She is the very model of a modern major Wolfean. I have added a short essay which originated in a different project, in which I was trying to chart a simplified history of the detective story genre. A major shift in the genre occurred, I think, in the 1970s, when the fictional detective became an engaged investigator: engaged at a personal level to a heterogeneous "family" and at a political level to the ideological commitments that set him or her in opposition to what the writer saw as the prevailing prejudices of the time. One obstacle to any simplified plan is the Notable Exception. Stout, I discovered, was a Notable Exception. He had Nero Wolfe doing in the 1940s and 1950s what I was arguing became the generic paradigm in the 1970s. I did what any manly simplifier would do; I downplayed the Exception. Here, I want to acknowledge it. Stout's sense of family and his political principles were, in significant ways, different from those which came to define the genre in the last decades of the century, and it is doubtful, in fact, that he was a direct influence. It was Hammett and Chandler who most often inspired later detective story writers. But Nero Wolfe's unorthodox family and his explicit political pronouncements were prophetic. Rex Stout was one of the first to exploit these themes. And he is still one of the best.

—J.K. Van Dover
January 2003

Author's Note:

Even though plot is not primary in a Stout mystery, care has been taken not to ruin any surprises. Murderers are not identified as such, nor are victims who die in the final third of the story. It is, however, only fair to warn keen-eyed readers that my essay, "Family, the Heron, and Senator McCarthy" (page 91) does, in passing, narrow the list of suspects in *A Family Affair* to a degree that might disappoint those who prefer only to work with what Archie reports.

CHRONOLOGY

1886 Rex Todhunter Stout born December 1st at Noblesville, Indiana, the sixth child of John Wallace Stout and Lucetta Todhunter.

1887 The Stouts move to Wakarusa, Kansas, later settling in Belleview (1896) and Topeka (1899). As a nine-year-old, Rex tours Kansas schools as a mathematical prodigy.

1905 Rex Stout joins the Navy, serving as pay yeoman on Theodore Roosevelt's presidential yacht.

1909 Stout settles in New York City.

1910 Makes his first professional sale, the poem "In Cupid's Family," to *Smart Set* (published November).

1912 Begins a stint as a writer for the new pulp magazines, making his first professional sale of a short story, "Excess Baggage," to *Short Stories* (published October). In the next four years, Stout publishes thirty-two stories and four novels.

1913 *Her Forbidden Knight*, Stout's first novel, is serialized in *All-Story Magazine* (August-December issues).

1916 Marries Fay Kennedy. With his brother, Bob (John Robert Stout), founds the Educational Thrift Service, a savings system for American school children; the venture is enormously successful.

1926 Now financially secure, he leaves ETS on his fortieth birthday.

1929 Stout's first serious novel (and first book), *How Like a God*, is published by Vanguard Press. Begins to build High Meadow, his home on the New York-Connecticut border.

1930 Publishes *Seed on the Wind*, a second mainstream novel.

1931 Divorces Fay Kennedy. *Golden Remedy* is published.

1932 Marries Pola Weinbach Hoffman, a designer of woolen fabrics.

1933 First daughter, Barbara, born Oct. 5th. *Forest Fire* is published.

1934 Publishes his first thriller, *The President Vanishes,* and the first Nero Wolfe novel, *Fer-de Lance* (October).

1935 *O Careless Love!,* a fifth mainstream novel, and *The League of Frightened Men,* the second Nero Wolfe book, are released.

1936 *The Rubber Band* published.

1937 Second daughter, Rebecca, born May 4th. *The Red Box* and *The Hand in the Glove* are published.

1938 *Mr. Cinderella* and *Too Many Cooks* are published.

1939 A banner year: *Some Buried Caesar, Mountain Cat, Double for Death,* and *Red Threads* are published.

1940 Publishes *Over My Dead Body, Where There's a Will,* and *Bad for Business.*

1941 Helps found the Fight for Freedom Committee, and Freedom House. Publishes *The Broken Vase* and *Alphabet Hicks,* the last novel not featuring Nero Wolfe.

1942 Stout is appointed Head of the Writers' War Board; as part of his war effort, he moderates a radio program, "Our Secret Weapon" (on CBS). Edits *The Illustrious Dunderheads,* and publishes *Black Orchids.*

1945 As President of the Authors' League, Stout campaigns for increased royalties for writers.

1946 Edits *Rue Morgue No. 1,* and publishes *The Silent Speaker.*

1949 Organizes the Writers' Board for World Government. Beginning this year, settles into a routine of producing two Wolfe books a year: a novel and a collection of three novellas.

1951 As president of the Authors' League, Stout condemns McCarthyism. Publishes *Curtains for Three* and *Murder by the Book.*

1954 Publishes *Three Men Out* and *The Black Mountain,* in which Nero Wolfe ventures to his native Montenegro.

1956 Edits *Eat, Drink, and Be Buried* (anthology), and publishes *Three Witnesses* and *Might As Well Be Dead.*

1964 With the short fiction market diminishing, Stout publishes *Trio for Blunt Instruments,* the last of the Wolfe novella collections.

1969 *Death of a Dude,* set on a Montana ranch, is published.

1973 Publishes *Please Pass the Guilt,* the first new Wolfe novel in four years.

1975 Publishes *A Family Affair,* the last Wolfe novel. Shortly thereafter, Rex Stout dies October 27th at his home, High Meadow.

1977 *Justice Ends at Home,* a collection of stories written by Stout for the pulps, is edited by John J. McAleer for Viking Press. McAleer's definitive biography, *Rex Stout,* is published by Little, Brown.

1980 A definitive primary and secondary bibliography by McAleer and Guy Townsend is published by Greenwood Press.

1985 Two posthumous Stout books appear: *Death Times Three,* uncollected stories, and *Under the Andes,* the first book publication of a lost-race adventure serialized in 1914.

Numerical Reference List
of Synopses

Alphabetical Reference List
of Synopses

I.

NERO WOLFE

INTRODUCTION

The fictional detective is usually a creature of some extravagance. He deliberately distinguishes himself from the common lot of humanity: he may be a bohemian or a lord, a ruffian or a fop, a recluse or a cosmopolitan, a blind man or a spinster. And he is also extravagant in the most literal sense: he is an extraordinary vagrant who roams through his world seeking truth in the streets of the city or the walks of a country estate. It is entirely appropriate that the reader first meets C. Auguste Dupin, the prototypical detective, roaming the midnight avenues of Paris in "The Murders in the Rue Morgue." The detective is a missionary who moves from one tragic scene to another, revealing moral reality and dispensing justice through the application of the gospel of his sect—be it that of ratiocination, intuition, forensic science, police procedure, or mere dogged persistence.

Nero Wolfe, the 270-pound devotee of orchids, is certainly extravagant in the primary sense. He consciously cultivates the art of abnormality. In his first published case, he proclaims to Archie, "I understand the technique of eccentricity; it would be futile for a man to labor at establishing a reputation for oddity if he were ready at the slightest provocation to revert to normal action" *(Fer-de-Lance,* Chapter 5). The particular oddity he is defending here is one of his most arbitrary: his refusal to conduct any business until the hour of eleven. In this instance, the district attorney of Westchester County had made the mistake of demanding Wolfe's cooperation at a quarter to eight. Throughout his career, Wolfe successfully maintains his inflexible schedule: breakfast at eight; the plant rooms from nine to eleven; business from eleven to lunch; two more hours with his orchids from four to six.

Wolfe is also a gourmet, employing a master chef, Fritz Brenner, in his kitchen. He is a prominent collector of orchids, employing Theodore Horstmann to supervise the ten thousand orchids raised in a rooftop greenhouse. Wolfe drinks six quarts of beer a day; he does not permit

1

the word "contact" to be used as a verb in his presence. He maintains an uncompromising set of prejudices: against women generally and hysterical women especially, against Germans (during World War II), against J. Edgar Hoover, against Richard Nixon (during Watergate), against the third edition of Webster's unabridged dictionary, against radio (and later against television).

But Wolfe's most extravagant distinction is his extreme antipathy to literal extravagance. He will not move. He insists upon the point: under no circumstances will he leave his home or violate his routines in order to facilitate an investigation. The exceptions are few and remarkable. Instead of spreading the principles of order and justice throughout his society, Wolfe imposes them dogmatically and absolutely within the walls of his house—the brownstone on West Thirty-Fifth Street—and he invites those who are troubled by an incomprehensible and threatening environment to enter the controlled economy of the house and to discover there the source of disorder in their own lives.

The invitation is extended to readers as well as to clients. The attraction of the detective story always lies in part in the reassuring message that the ways of the world are not accidental and meaningless. The argument of every story affirms that the death of an individual is the consequence of a plot and that the outlines of that plot may be discerned retrospectively by the detective. The character of the detective's intelligence is not supernatural, but is nearly infallible. The detective stands as a modern—i.e., a rational, scientific-surrogate for God. Wolfe's vaunted immobility symbolizes this function. He is virtually a parody of Aristotle's definition of God: the Unmoved Mover.

In *Fer-de-Lance*, Archie visits Wolfe's bedroom (to report DA Anderson's ill-timed arrival) and finds the detective reclining on his canopied bed beneath black silk curtains and sheets. "Inside it on the white pillow his big fat face reposed like an image in a temple." Wolfe's face—and the brain behind it—radiates moral intelligence against a black background of the apparent chaos of modern life. Wolfe's affectation of yellow garments—especially his canary yellow silk pajamas—completes the suggestion that he represents a fixed, Apollonian sun in the middle of a dark, Dionysiac universe of passion, shadow, and death.

This then comprises the essential appeal of the Wolfe series. Stout invented his morally active, physically inert agent at a time of social crisis. Prohibition had undermined confidence in legislated morality and the Depression had shaken faith in the economic system. Evidence of those challenges to the social structure appears in the backgrounds of the early Wolfe novels. The confident certainties of Wolfe's exploits served as an antidote to the pressing uncertainties of the real world. Indeed, Wolfe's investigations are continually set in the context of contemporary American history. World War II ("Not Quite Dead Enough," "Booby Trap"), industrial ethics (*The Silent Speaker*), communism and anti-communism (*The Second Confession*, "Home to Roost"), wiretapping and invasions of privacy ("Too Many Detectives," *The Doorbell Rang*), civil rights (*A Right to Die*), feminism (*Please Pass the Guilt*), Watergate (*A Family Affair*)—all touch Wolfe's world, and all are dramatically subordinated to his unfailing investigations into good and evil.

That readers have proved endlessly fascinated with the topography of Wolfe's brownstone temple should not be surprising. In response to many inquiries, Stout had printed diagrams of the arrangement of the ground floor. Wolfe's haven is a sort of heaven, a place where the will—rational (godly) and whimsical (human)—of a benign divinity asserts itself unequivocally. It is the center from which moral order emanates, and the details of its layout and its operations are signs of its stability. For forty years, Wolfe prepares menus with Fritz and pots orchids with Theodore. For forty years, Archie takes notes at his desk, the client sits in the red chair and the other principals distribute themselves in the yellow chairs, and Wolfe presides from his custom-made throne. For forty years, Inspector Cramer and Sergeant Purley Stebbins ring the doorbell, enter the office, and explode with indignation at Wolfe's intractability. The front room, the elevator, the three-foot globe—all persist in place through forty years of American history. Wolfe's roadster may become a sedan (though it remains a Heron), but inside the house, the furnishings are permanent. Like Holmes's 221B Baker Street, Wolfe's West Thirty-Fifth Street remains a fixed point in a turning world. Hence the utter outrage of the FBI black bag intrusion in *The Doorbell Rang*. Hence the astonishment shared by Archie and the reader when Wolfe, in his grand struggle with his Napoleon of Crime, Arnold Zeck, flees the brownstone and—in what Stout admitted to be a deliberate symbol—leaves the door open (*In the Best Families*).

The intrinsic interest attached to the divisions of time and space in Wolfe's private world perhaps encouraged Stout in the tendency toward a slightly mechanical execution of the narrative in the later novels. If reassuring repetition was what the readers desired—an adult version of the child's insistence upon invariability in the telling of a fairy tale—sometimes that was all that they got. Stout seems to be almost absent-mindedly rocking the cradle in some of the late novels. But early or late, the eccentric world of Nero Wolfe emphasizes the extraordinary control of an extraordinary individual, a demi-god of ratiocination dominating his personal temple of dogmatisms.

Wolfe's oddities and his overwhelming intellect align him with the traditional school of fictional detectives, the Holmeses, the Wimseys, and the Vances. But his debut coincided with the introduction of a new species of detective, the hardboiled private eye, who emerged as a popular type in America in the late twenties and early thirties, and who tended to be defiantly commonplace. The private eye solved his cases through a combination of forcefulness (fist and gun), endurance, and perseverance. Once he has committed himself to a case, Wolfe perseveres; but he exerts no force and needs endure only fools. Nonetheless, Stout managed cleverly to incorporate the new trend in detectives in the person of Wolfe's assistant, Archie Goodwin.

Archie is at least semi-tough. Only once (in *The Red Box*) is he involved in the third-degree brutality which characterizes the hardboiled novel. Less violent than his fellow private eyes, Archie is, like them, a peripatetic wise guy. Wolfe has the *savoir faire;* Archie has the street smarts. He is the one who must venture out to bring the errant worldlings into Wolfe's temple of justice for correction. And he is the one who does most of the enduring and the persevering. He is frequently jailed for refusing to cooperate with the authorities, and one of his primary responsibilities consists in regularly prodding Wolfe to undertake (*i.e.,* to prescribe) some action.

Archie's voice is the vehicle through which the action is conveyed. This is another trait he shares with the hardboiled hero. When the traditional detective story employs a first-person narrator, he is a dull and decent Watson, awed by the penetration of his companion. Archie is sharp and self-assertive. He respects Wolfe, but he also assumes that the best New York detective living outside Wolfe's brownstone is the third best detective in the city. Nor is Archie a naive partisan of the establishment. Though he never embraces the cynicism endemic to the tough guy posture, he is a social critic. A strain of skeptical Huckleberry Finnism runs through his character and even expresses itself in his language. In the following instance, it extends into his relationship with Wolfe:

> There was no use trying to get Wolfe to pull up a little; I hardly ever wasted time on that any more. If I undertook to explain how easy he might be wrong he would just say,
> "You know a fact when you see it, Archie, but you have no feeling for phenomena." After I had looked up the word phenomena in the dictionary I couldn't see that he had anything, but there was no use arguing with him.

Archie's inexhaustible fluency is one of the principal pleasures of the series. Wolfe withdraws from experience in order to explain it; Archie plunges into experience and conveys the excitement of his involvement in the raciness of his prose.

Wolfe, by contrast, tends to be urbane and epigrammatic. Especially in the first half dozen novels, his authority embodies itself in his very syntax. His magisterial pronouncements are marvelous.

You know, Mr. Townsend, it is our good fortune that the exigencies of birth and training furnish all of us with opportunities for snobbery. My ignorance of this special nomenclature provided yours; your innocence of the elementary mental processes provides mine.

Skepticism is a good watchdog if you know when to take the leash off.

It is always wiser, when there is a choice, to trust to inertia. It is the greatest force in the world.

The essence of sainthood is expiation.

I understand your contention: that a point arrives when finesse must retire and leave the *coup de grace* for naked force.

—All from *Fer-de-Lance*

If Archie's voice represents a witty, spontaneous response to the events of his experience, Wolfe's aphoristic style represents his ability to shape and control events. Returning to the image of the detective as divinity, Wolfe's mastery of language signifies his recreative word. God said, Let there be Light, and there was Light. The detective is not quite God; his words cannot create light, but they can cast it. He can use language to reconstruct events and thus expose the meaningful plot which underlies them. Wolfe is one of the most verbal of detectives. His investigative technique inevitably involves gathering the principals in his office and subjecting them to an enlightening cross-examination. Through his artful phrasings and fabrications, Wolfe works his way to statements of the truth.

Rex Stout's place in the top rank of mystery writers is secure. Others have been more inventive at devising effective plots; others have more fully realized the social settings of the crimes; others have created more interesting and distinctive victims, criminals, and suspects. But few have produced such a fascinating set of continuing characters or written about them with such consistent elegance. Nero Wolfe, Archie Goodwin, and the repertory cast of supporting players performed magnificently for forty years. The record of their achievement is a permanent contribution to literature.

SYNOPSES

Repertory Cast

Nero Wolfe and **Archie Goodwin:** Detectives.

Fritz Brenner: Wolfe's Swiss master chef and major domo.

Theodore Horstmann: Wolfe's resident orchidologist.

Marko Vukcic: Wolfe's best friend; a fellow Montenegrin refugee; proprietor of the world-renowned Rusterman's Restaurant; assassinated in *The Black Mountain*.

Saul Panzer; Fred Durkin; Orrie Cather; Johnny Keems; Bill Gore: free-lance detectives employed by Wolfe on various occasions to assist him in his investigations. He calls most regularly upon the trio of Panzer, Durkin, and Cather.

Inspector Cramer: ubiquitous, cigar-chewing, fat-rumped head of the Homicide Bureau. First name "Fergus" in *Where There's A Will;* first initials "L. T." in *The Silent Speaker*.

Purley Stebbins: Sergeant in the Homicide Bureau.

Lily Rowan: wealthy daughter of a New York City sewer czar; Archie's steady companion after 1938 (*Some Buried Caesar*).

Lon Cohen: well-placed reporter on *The Gazette;* an invariably useful source of confidential information.

Nathaniel Parker: Wolfe's lawyer.

Doc Vollmer: Wolfe's doctor.

THE STORIES

1. *Fer-de-Lance* (1934)

Victims: Carlo Maffei—immigrant metal-worker; knifed. Peter Oliver Barstow—President of Holland College; poisoned.

Clients: Maria Maffei—sister of Carlo. Ellen Barstow—deranged widow of Peter.

Other Principals: Anna Fiore—cleaning girl at Carlo Maffei's boarding house. Sarah Barstow—daughter of Peter and Ellen. Lawrence Barstow—son and member of foursome at father's death. E. D. Kimball—financier and member of foursome. Manuel Kimball—son of E. D. and member of foursome.

Synopsis: Maria Maffei consults Wolfe regarding the disappearance of her brother. Information derived from Anna Fiore leads Wolfe to connect Carlo with Peter Oliver Barstow's apparently accidental death on a golf course. He provokes an official reinvestigation of the case. This leads to the discovery of a poisoned needle. The widow offers a large reward, and this becomes Wolfe's incentive. He exposes a red herring laid by the Barstow family physician and concludes that Barstow was not the intended target. The murderer attempts to kill Wolfe with a poisonous snake (a Fer-de-Lance). Then, warned by Wolfe of impending arrest, the murderer kills the original target and commits suicide.

Comment: The basic conventions are all in evidence—Wolfe's obesity, immobility, daily routines, elegant diction. Panzer, Durkin, Cather, and Gore debut in supporting roles. Wolfe and Archie engage in typical squabbles; Wolfe is gratuitously and offensively curt to certain callers, and is an irresistibly pleasant host to others. His ethical standards are unusually idiosyncratic. Many fictional detectives permit or encourage the villain to commit suicide; Wolfe virtually encourages the murderer to carry out the originally intended killing. Wolfe offers a sentimental excuse for his action; Archie suspects that his motive was to avoid a subpoena to the murderer's trial.

There are signs of the times: movies cost twenty cents, and Archie alludes to the Lindbergh kidnaping and to New York Giants manager John J. McGraw. The Depression and Prohibition are present in the background, and Archie feels free to refer to a South American as a "spiggoty. "

2. *The League of Frightened Men* (1935)

Victims: William R. Harrison—judge; fall from a cliff. Eugene Dreyer—art dealer; poisoned. Andrew Hibbard—psychologist; vanished. Loring A. Burton—doctor; shot.

Clients: "The League of Frightened Men": Andrew Hibbard, Leopold Elkus (surgeon), Loring A. Burton, Augustus Farrell (architect), Ferdinand Bowen (stockbroker), Michael Ayers (newspaperman), Pitney Scott (taxi driver), Nicholas Cabot (lawyer), and other members of "The League." Evelyn Hibbard—daughter of Andrew Hibbard.

Other Principals: Paul Chapin—playwright and novelist. Dora Chapin—Paul's wife.

Synopsis: The League of Frightened Men (formerly The League of Atonement) consists of a group of Harvard classmates implicated in a prank which resulted in the crippling of Paul Chapin. They seek to atone by supporting the writer financially. Harrison and Dreyer die, the one apparently by accident, the other apparently a suicide. Hibbard disappears. After each event, Chapin sends the members a poem intimating his responsibility. The League employs Wolfe to prevent further deaths. Wolfe conducts a series of interviews in his office. Burton dies. Wolfe discovers the fate of Hibbard. In a climactic scene, Wolfe gathers together in his office all the principals and reveals the identity of the criminal.

Comment: One of the best-plotted of the novels. None of the office scenes suffers from implausibly forced attendances. The climactic scene is the first of many in which Wolfe exposes the truth by gathering all of the principals in his office and artfully conducting his questioning. Wolfe protests that identifying the killer matters less to him than fulfilling his contract and being paid.

The psychopathology of the damaged, pitied, imaginative writer, Chapin, makes for an unusually interesting character study. Otherwise, the novel confirms all of the standard conventions of the series. The effects of the Depression are suggested when Harvard alumni appear as unemployed architects, alcoholic newspapermen, and taxi drivers (making $18.50 per week).

3. *The Rubber Band* (1936)

Victim: Harlan Scovill—rancher and member of the Rubber Band; shot.

Client: Clara Fox—daughter of Gilbert Fox, member of the Rubber Band.

Other Principals: Anthony D. Perry—multi-millionaire President of Seaboard Products. Ramsey Muir—vice-president of Seaboard Products. Michael Walsh—member of the Rubber Band. Hilda Lindquist—daughter of Victor Lindquist, member of the Rubber Band. Marquis of Clivers—wealthy English nobleman and diplomat. Francis Horrocks—aide to the Marquis.

Synopsis: Anthony Perry consults Wolfe regarding the theft of $30,000 from his company. Clara Fox, an employee, is the prime suspect. The same evening Clara visits Wolfe in the company of Mike Walsh and Hilda Lindquist. She tells the story of the Rubber Band, a gang of young men in Silver City, Nevada to which her father belonged in the 1890s. An Englishman whom the gang aided had promised half of his inheritance to its members. Clara has recognized the Marquis of Clivers, in America on a delicate diplomatic mission, as the Englishman. Harlan Scovill, on his way to Wolfe's to join the evening meeting, is gunned down on the streets. Wolfe accepts Clara as a client and conceals her in his house. He inquires into the matter of the theft and into that of the Marquis. A second associate of the Band is killed. Wolfe gathers the remaining principals in his office and identifies the killer. The murderer is killed while attempting to shoot Wolfe (who suffers a flesh wound to the arm).

Comment: The Rubber Band supplies a melodramatic background to the action—cowboys, noblemen, jailbreaks, disguised identities. The characters are colorful, and the romantic subplot is inoffensive.

    Another background—one of international instability—is alluded to by Inspector Cramer: "You know how it is nowadays, everybody's got it in for somebody else, and half of them have gone cuckoo. When a German ship lands here a bunch of Jews go and tear the flag off it and raise general hell. If a Wop professor that's been kicked out of Italy tries to give a lecture here a gang of Fascists haul him down and beat him up. When you try your best to feed people that haven't got a job they turn Communist on you and start a riot." Lieutenant Rowcliff's legal ransacking of Wolfe's brownstone in a search for Clara epitomizes this general atmosphere of bullying and turmoil. Wolfe's confident solution of the mystery stands for the rational alternative to violence.

4. *The Red Box* (1937)

Victims: Molly Lauck—fashion model; poisoned. Boyden McNair—designer of women's woolen garments; poisoned.

Client: Helen Frost—fashion model and heiress.

Other Principals: Calida Frost—mother of Helen. Dudley Frost—uncle of Helen. Llewellyn Frost—son of Dudley and ortho-cousin of Helen. Thelma Mitchell—friend of Helen. Perren Gebert—friend of the Frosts with NVMS (No Visible Means of Support).

Synopsis: Llewellyn Frost requires Wolfe to investigate the death of Molly Lauck, and actually gets the detective to visit the scene of the crime. Unable to secure the cooperation of any of the principals, Wolfe forces information from Helen Frost. Boyden McNair calls upon Wolfe to inform him that he has appointed Wolfe his executor. As he is about to explain the significance of the red box, McNair suddenly dies. Helen now employs Wolfe to investigate the death of McNair, whom she has always regarded fondly. Wolfe discovers a complex set of family relations. At the funeral of McNair, another of the principals is poisoned. Having deduced the murderer, Wolfe has Inspector Cramer gather the remaining principals in his office and uses a trick to confirm his conclusions. The murderer commits suicide.

Comment: Wolfe is at his formidable best. Though the plot is partly improbable and partly obvious, the characters and the dialogue are sharp. Archie subordinates himself to a cast of strong, weak, voluble, sardonic, sentimental, exploitative individuals.

    The police resort to a rather brutal third degree when questioning Perren Gebert, the only such hardboiled incident in the series.

5. *Too Many Cooks* (1938)

Victim: Phillip Laszio—master chef; stabbed.

Client: Jerome Berin—master chef.

Other Principals: Dina Laszio—"swamp woman" (Archie's phrase) and wife of Phillip. Marko Vukcic—master chef and former husband of Dina Laszio. Domenico Rossi—master chef and father of Dina Laszio. Leon Blanc—master chef, supplanted by Phillip Laszio. Louis Servan—master chef and host of Les Quinze Maîtres. Ramsey Keith, Pierre Mondor, Lawrence Coyne, Sergei Vallenko—master chefs. Raymond

Ligget—owner of The Churchill, Lazio's restaurant. Constanza Berin—daughter of Jerome. Barry Tolman—prosecuting attorney, Marlin County, West Virginia.

Synopsis: The action takes place in Kanawha Spa, West Virginia, at the convocation of a select group of master chefs from around the world, Les Quinze Maîtres. Wolfe has been invited as guest of honor. His primary motive for making the excursion is to obtain Jerome Berin's secret recipe for *saucisse minuit*, which he had tasted as a youth in Catalonia. Phillip Laszio, disliked for a variety of reasons by his fellow maîtres, is killed while presiding over an extraordinary sauce-tasting. Suspicion falls upon Berin, but Wolfe convinces the prosecutor that the killer wore blackface. The murderer attempts to assassinate Wolfe, who suffers a flesh wound. Wolfe now sets out in earnest to identify a killer. He succeeds by breaking down an alibi. Jerome Berin reluctantly concedes to the demands of gratitude and shares the secret of *saucisse minuit*.

Comment: The occasion of Wolfe's brief foray beyond the walls of his brownstone produces an unusual variety of characters and a very unusual non-urban setting. It also results in the fullest portrait of his gastronomical interests. The chefs are all temperamental artists, and there is much incidental discussion of the fine points of gourmet cooking. Wolfe delivers a formal address on the supremacy of native American cuisine.

Race relations become an issue. Archie, prosecutor Tolman, and Sheriff Pettigrew casually employ denigrative epithets—nigger, smoke, boy, African, pickaninny. Wolfe condescends to the black service staff no more than he does to anyone else, and he even surprises one of the waiters, Paul Whipple, by citing a line from Paul Laurence Dunbar. Tolman and Pettigrew protest Wolfe's misguided decency.

Tolman figures in a humorous subplot romance with Constanza Berin. The novel ends with Archie's amusing gesture to reconcile them.

6. *Some Buried Caesar* (1939)

Victims: Clyde Osgood—scion of a wealthy upstate family; gored. Howard Bronson—owed $10,000 by Clyde; pitchforked.

Client: Frederick Osgood—father of Clyde.

Other Principals: Thomas Pratt—proprietor of a chain of "Pratterias" and rival of Frederick Osgood. Jimmy—son of Thomas and linked with Nancy Osgood and Lily Rowan. Caroline Pratt—daughter of Thomas.

Nancy—daughter of Frederick. Lily Rowan—object of Jimmy Pratt's infatuation. Monte McMillan—former owner of Caesar. Hickory Caesar Grindon—a $45,000 Guernsey bull.

Synopsis: A tire blow-out as Archie is driving Wolfe to the North Atlantic Exposition in Crowfield (where he intends to humiliate a fellow orchid collector at an exhibition) causes Wolfe to accept the hospitality of Thomas Pratt. As a publicity stunt, Pratt has purchased a prize bull, Caesar, to barbecue for selected guests at his farm. Clyde Osgood, whose family regards Pratt as an upstart neighbor, bets that Caesar will never be eaten. That night Clyde's mangled body is found in Caesar's field. Wolfe proves that the bull was not the killer, and Osgood hires him to find the actual murderer. Caesar dies of anthrax. At the Exposition (where Wolfe's plants win the medal and three ribbons), Archie finds the body of Bronson and spends a night in jail as a material witness. Wolfe obtains his release. During a private interview with the murderer Wolfe receives a signed confession; he then allows the killer to commit suicide.

Comment: As in *Too Many Cooks*, the action takes place entirely outside Wolfe's brownstone; and, as in the previous novel, it depends in part upon specialized knowledge (there, haute cuisine; here, the rating and registering of bulls). Wolfe is formidable; Archie is fresh. Though there are signs that the characters are sliding into obvious stereotypes, the contrast between the old money of the Osgoods and the brash new money of the Pratts is effective (Pratt: "Last week we served a daily average of 42,392 lunches in Greater New York at an average cost to the consumer of twenty-three and seventeen-hundredths cents"). There is little attention to details of manners, psychology, or setting.

Archie acquires Lily Rowan, the vampish daughter of a millionaire builder of sewers. She has just cast off Jimmy Pratt and is destined to be Archie's principal female interest throughout the series. Here he plays hard to get.

7. *Over My Dead Body* (1940)

Victims: Percy Ludlow—British undercover agent; stabbed with an *épée*. Rudolph Faber—German undercover agent; stabbed with a pocket knife.

Client: Neya Tormic (alias)—Wolfe's adopted Croatian daughter.

Other Principals: Carla Lovchen—Croatian companion of Neya Tormic. Nikola and Jeanne Miltan—proprietors of a fencing emporium. Nat Driscoll—student of fencing. Madame Zorka—Fifth Avenue couturière and student of fencing. John P. Barrett—New York financier. Donald Barrett—son of John P. and a student of fencing.

Synopsis: When Neya Tormic, a fencing instructor at Miltan's, is accused of stealing jewels from Nat Driscoll, she calls upon her adoptive father for assistance. The robbery proves to be a misunderstanding, but just as Archie finishes his brief investigation, one of Neya's fencing partners—Percy Ludlow—is found dead. Wolfe becomes aware of international complications involving the unstable politics of the Balkans. Rudolph Faber is found murdered in the apartment shared by Neya and Carla Lovchen. Inspector Cramer confesses himself baffled by the political implications. Wolfe discovers that the conspiracy centers on the incognito presence in New York of the Croatian princess, Vladanka Donevitch. The princess plans to ally her people with the Nazis. As Wolfe discloses the identity of the murderer to Inspector Cramer, he is attacked and himself kills the criminal with two beer bottles.

Comment: Little effort is made to anchor the political intrigues in reality. It merely serves to provide an unsophisticated and melodramatic motivation for the crimes. It does, at least, allow Wolfe to dramatize his convictions with regard to politics (anti-Nazi, and he admits to making contributions to the Loyalist cause in Spain), financiers ("When an international financier is confronted by a holdup man with a gun, he automatically hands over not only his money and jewelry but also his shirt and pants, because it doesn't occur to him that a robber might draw a line somewhere"), and his clients (he insists that they be innocent). It also provides further information about Wolfe's family and background.

The fencing school is *outré* but, like the politics, nonessential. Archie needlessly absconds with the first murder weapon; Wolfe needlessly withholds it by concealing it in a chocolate covered loaf of Italian bread. Cramer cooperates humbly with Wolfe's irregularity. Wolfe encounters his first G-Man, Mr. Stahl of the FBI, a humorously mechanical bureaucrat. The first half dozen Wolfe novels established the detective as an original creation. *Over My Dead Body* begins the long line of pleasant entertainments in which Wolfe and Archie exploit the familiar formulas.

Wolfe declares to Mr. Stahl that he is by birth an American. Stout later explained that this statement was forced upon him by his editors. On all other occasions Wolfe affirms his Montenegrin origins.

8. *Where There's a Will* (1940)

Victims: Noel Hawthorne—self-made multi-millionaire; shot. Naomi Karn—woman friend of Noel, and his heir; strangled.

Clients: April Hawthorne—actress and sister of Noel. May Hawthorne—college president and sister of Noel. June Hawthorne Dunn—author and sister of Noel. Daisy Hawthorne—wife of Noel and veiled to conceal injured face. John Charles Dunn—U.S. Secretary of State and husband of June.

Other Principals: Sara Dunn—amateur photographer and daughter of June. Andy Dunn—son of June. Glenn Prescott—Hawthorne family lawyer. Eugene Davis—Prescott's law partner and lover of Naomi. Osric Stauffer—companion of April. Celia Fleet—aide to April.

Synopsis: The Hawthorne sisters and their lawyer consult Wolfe regarding their brother's will, which has left the bulk of his estate to Naomi Kam. To satisfy the demands of Daisy, they employ Wolfe to negotiate with Naomi in order to achieve a fairer distribution of the wealth. The police discover that Noel's death was not accidental. Wolfe undertakes to investigate the crime; he and Archie question the family members at the Hawthorne mansion in Manhattan. Archie discovers the body of Naomi. A series of photos taken by Sara provide Wolfe with a clue. Inspector Cramer threatens to hold Wolfe as a material witness, but Wolfe convinces him to gather all the principals in Wolfe's office, where he dramatically exposes the murderer.

Comment: The cast is large, but the possibilities—the veiled Daisy, passion-inspiring Naomi, imperious May, languid April, etc.—are not fully developed. Wolfe's clients now arrive with foreknowledge of his routines. May predicts his 4:00 p.m. departure to his orchids. Wolfe's idiosyncrasies seem more mechanical, and his willfulness seems closer to arrogance. He responds with contempt to Inspector Cramer's warrant for his arrest.

The story opens with references to the WPA and the turmoil in Europe, but the events of the case transpire entirely in the isolated and secure environment of Wolfe's brownstone and the Dunn and Hawthorne estates.

9. "Bitter End" (November, 1940)

Victim: Arthur Tingley—head of Tingley's Tidbits; slashed throat.

Clients: Leonard Cliff—vice president of P & B (Provisions and Beverages). Amy Duncan—Tingley's niece and Cliff's secretary.

Other Principals: Gwendolyn Yates—Tingley's chief assistant. Carrie Murphy—assistant to Miss Yates. Philip Tingley—Arthur's adopted son. Guthrie Judd—wealthy banker and promoter of Consolidated Cereals. Martha Judd—Guthrie's sister.

Synopsis: Wolfe discovers that someone has "poisoned" his liver *paté* with quinine and he vows to apprehend the perpetrator. Coincidentally, Amy Duncan, niece of the *paté's* manufacturer, calls upon Wolfe to ask him to investigate the sabotage of her uncle's product. Archie discovers the dead Tingley and the unconscious Amy in an office of the firm's Manhattan factory. Leonard Cliff attacks Archie in a mistaken effort to protect Amy, then hires Wolfe to investigate the crime on her behalf. Wolfe discovers a complex plot involving the paternity of Philip Tingley. He gathers all of the principals in his office and exposes the murderer.

Comment: The novella has a curious history. Stout had originally composed the story as a Tecumseh Fox novel, *Bad for Business. The American Magazine* offered to double his fee if he would convert it to a Nero Wolfe tale. The original version, with Fox as the detective, was also published in book form in November 1940. "Bitter End" was first published in hardcover in the posthumous limited edition tribute to Rex Stout, *Corsage: A Bouquet of Rex Stout and Nero Wolfe* (1977). "Bitter End" was later reprinted as part of the last compiled Wolfe novella trilogy, *Death Times Three* (1985).

"Bitter End" is a competent, conventional mystery, with a more than usual amount of blood, fisticuffs, and plot intricacies. The initial scene, in which Wolfe spits a mouthful of the unpalatable *paté* in Archie's face, is a memorable one.

10. "Black Orchids"
in *Black Orchids* (1942)

Victim: Harry Gould—employee of W. G. Dill; shot.

Client: Lewis Hewitt—horticulturalist and breeder of black orchids

Other Principals: W. G. Dill—horticulturalist. Fred Updegraff—horticulturalist. Anne Tracy—employee of W. G. Dill. Rose Lasher—friend of Harry Gould.

Synopsis: Wolfe attends the Flower Show at the Grand Central Palace, and covets the black orchids exhibited by Lewis Hewitt. W. G. Dill uses two models, Harry Gould and Anne Tracy, to draw attention to his exhibit. Gould, apparently asleep in the bucolic stage setting, is discovered to be dead, and Wolfe and Archie realize that a gesture of Archie's actually fired the weapon that killed Gould. Hewitt is also circumstantially implicated in the crime. Wolfe demands the black orchids as his fee for investigating the situation. The plot centers on the disagreeable personality of Gould and involves blackmail, plant poisonings, and broken romances. Wolfe gathers the principals (including Inspector Cramer) in his own flower rooms and, employing a stratagem, presents enough proof to cause the murderer to commit unintentional suicide.

Comment: The early novellas, like the early novels, are the best. Wolfe's covetousness and Archie's infatuation (with Anne Tracy) are finely presented. The setting is distinctive and the execution of the murder is original. The death is unusually realistic: Archie probes Gould's head wound—"I reached a hand to feel of it, and the end of my finger went right into a hole in his skull, away in, and it was like sticking your finger into a warm apple pie." Wolfe serves *saucisse minuit*, the recipe of which he had extorted from Jerome Berin in *Too Many Cooks*. Here he satisfies his other sensual appetite by extorting the unique orchids from Lewis Hewitt.

11. "Cordially Invited to Meet Death"
in *Black Orchids* (1942)

Victim: Bess Huddleston—society hostess; poisoned.

Client: Bess Huddleston.

Other Principals: Larry Huddleston—doltish nephew of Bess. Daniel Huddleston—chemist brother of Bess. Janet Nichols—assistant to Bess. Maryella Timms—secretary to Bess. Dr. Brady—friend of Bess.

Synopsis: Some of Bess Huddleston's peers have received notes suggesting (falsely) that she has been indiscreet. She hires Wolfe to discover the source of the libel. Archie visits the Huddleston estate—where alligators, bears, and chimpanzees roam freely—and while he is there Miss Huddleston cuts her toe. Three days later she dies of tetanus poisoning. The poison was contained in the antiseptic iodine. Janet Nichols is also poisoned, but receives the necessary anti-toxin. Wolfe gathers the principals in his office, sorts out a series of emotional entanglements, and deduces the identity of the killer.

Comment: Another well-crafted novella, in the eccentric-household tradition. There are a few incidental references to warfare, hinting at the World War II.

12. "Not Quite Dead Enough"
in *Not Quite Dead Enough* (1944)

Victim: Ann Amory—a girl with a problem; strangled.

Client: Archie Goodwin.

Other Principals: Lily Rowan—Archie's special friend and Ann's acquaintance. Mrs. Chack—Ann's grandmother. Miss Leeds—Ann's landlady. Roy Douglas—pigeon fancier and Ann's fiancé. Leon Furey—Ann's neighbor.

Synopsis: Archie, a major in Army Intelligence, is assigned the task of diverting Wolfe from his intention to lose weight and enlist in the regular army in order to "shoot Germans" (his civilian brain being of greater service to the nation in New York City). Archie learns from Lily that Ann has a problem which might interest Wolfe, but before he can investigate it, Ann is dead. Archie deliberately frames himself for the murder, thus forcing Wolfe to intervene in his defense. Wolfe questions the witnesses and identifies Ann's killer.

Comment: Wolfe's virulent anti-German sentiments (shared by Stout during the war) and his willingness to sacrifice his routines are noteworthy. His irrational bloodthirstiness is disquieting; one expects a more rational, pragmatic response from the detective.

13. "Booby Trap"
in *Not Quite Dead Enough* (1944)

Victims: Major Cross—military intelligence officer; defenestrated. Colonel Ryder—military intelligence officer; grenade explosion.

Client: U.S. Government.

Other Principals: General Carpenter—Chief of Military Intelligence. General Fife, Colonel Tinkham, Lieutenant Lawson, Sergeant Bruce—Military Intelligence staff. John Bell Shattuck—U.S. Congressman.

Synopsis: Wolfe and Military Intelligence are investigating war profiteering—the theft of patented ideas through a claim of military necessity. Congressman Shattuck has received a note suggesting that the death of one of the investigators, Major Cross, was not accidental. The briefcase of Colonel Ryder is booby-trapped with the prototype of a secret new grenade. Wolfe gathers the principals in his office and uses a psychological experiment to determine the identity of the murderer. In order to preserve morale, Wolfe prompts the killer to avoid a trial by committing suicide.

Comment: Wolfe has subordinated his eccentricities to the national interest: he eats within the limits of his ration coupons, he attends meetings outside his brownstone, he communes only irregularly with his orchids. He treats the military authorities with as much arrogance as he treated the civilian police.

14. *The Silent Speaker* (1946) 7 9 8

Victims: Cheney Boone—Director of the Bureau of Price Regulation (BPR); beaten. Phoebe Gunther—Boone's confidential secretary; beaten.

Client: National Industrial Association (NIA), comprised of businessmen worth, in aggregate, over thirty billion 1946 dollars.

Other Principals: Edward Frank Erskine—president, NIA. Donald O'Neill, Mr. Breslow, Mr. Winterhoff—members, NIA. Alger Kates—member of the Research Department, BPR. Solomon Dexter—acting director, BPR. Mrs. Boone—wife of Cheney Boone. Nina Boone—niece of Cheney Boone.

Synopsis: Boone's regulatory agency has been the nemesis of the NIA. His murder, which took place as he was preparing to deliver a speech to the NIA convention, has aroused public opinion against the NIA. Wolfe provokes the NIA into employing him to undertake an investigation. He twice gathers representatives from the NIA, the BPR, the NYPD, and the FBI in his office. On the second occasion, the body of Phoebe Gunther is found in an areaway outside the brownstone. The NIA suffers further embarrassment. Inspector Cramer is replaced by the offensive Inspector Ash. Wolfe repudiates his commission from the NIA, returning his $30,000 retainer. He holds himself incommunicado until forced to act; then he calls Inspector Cramer and selected individuals to his office and exposes a plot involving bribery and murder. Cramer arrests the killer and recovers his official position. Wolfe accepts a $100,000 reward from the NIA.

Comment: Wolfe's return to the novel-length mystery is a strong one: the plot is solid and the characters—especially Phoebe Gunther—are interesting. There are also strong ideological implications to the action. Miss Gunther refers to the capitalists of the NIA as "the dirtiest gang of pigs and chiselers on earth." Solomon Dexter calls them "the dirtiest bunch of liars and cutthroats in existence." Archie and Wolfe evidently share this estimation. Wolfe deliberately prolongs the public rancor against the NIA until events force him to disclose the criminal and to accept the NIA's gratitude and money.

15. *Too Many Women* (1947)

Victims: Waldo Wilmot Moore—correspondence checker at Naylor-Kerr; automobile accident. Kerr Naylor—ambitious, eccentric Naylor-Kerr heir; automobile accident.

Client: Naylor-Kerr, Inc.—major engineers' equipment and supplies firm.

Other Principals: Jasper Pine—president of Naylor-Kerr. Cecily Pine—wife of Jasper and eccentric Naylor-Kerr heir. Rosa Bendini, Hester Livsey, Gwynne Ferris—Naylor-Kerr secretaries and stenographers. Harold Anthony—husband of Rosa Bendini. Benjamin Frenkel, Summer Hoff, Mr. Rosenbaum—Naylor-Kerr employees.

Synopsis: Kerr Naylor has been unaccountably circulating a rumor that the apparent hit-and-run death of Waldo Moore was not an accident. On behalf of the corporation, Jasper Pine employs Wolfe to investigate the case. Archie spends several days exploring the oddities of the Naylor-Kerr stock department. Kerr Naylor is killed. Wolfe interviews several of the principals and decides upon a stratagem that requires Archie to spread a rumor. Wolfe's device bears fruit; he calls two crucial witnesses to his office and obtains the truth. The killer commits suicide before Wolfe can act.

Comment: *Too Many Women* is one of the last novels of the series to animate the established conventions without going beyond them (e.g., by introducing a master criminal or by implicating one of the members of the repertory cast). Wolfe's role is subordinate to that of Archie, who engages in a number of entertaining encounters with the women of Naylor-Kerr.

16. *And Be a Villain* (1948)

Victims: Cyril Orchard—editor of a race track tout sheet; poisoned. Beula Poole—editor of an economics/politics tout sheet; shot. Deborah Koppel—personal manager of Madeline Fraser; poisoned.

Clients: 50%—Hi-Spot, a soft drink company, Walter B. Anderson, president. 30%—FBC (Federal Broadcasting Company), a radio network. 15%—Madeline Fraser, radio talk show hostess. 5%—White Birch Soap.

Other Principals: Elinor Vance—researcher for Madeline Fraser. Nancylee Shepherd—teenage fan of Miss Fraser. Tully Strong—secretary of the Sponsor's Council. Nathan Traub—advertising executive. Professor F. O. Saverese—mathematician. Arnold Zeck—criminal mastermind.

Synopsis: Cyril Orchard, a guest on Madeline Fraser's show, is poisoned on the air when he drinks from a sponsor's product (Hi-Spot soda). Wolfe arranges to be employed by those affected by the bad publicity. He discovers that the poison may have been intended for Miss Fraser. He deduces from the coincidental death of Beula Poole that the tout sheets are part of a blackmail scheme. Arnold Zeck phones to warn Wolfe to proceed no further. Wolfe proceeds further. While on assignment at Miss Fraser's apartment, Archie witnesses the death of Deborah Koppel. Wolfe has the cooperative Cramer gather the principals in his office and through clever questioning discloses the identity of the murder.

Comment: This is the first of three Zeck novels. Stout has declared, "When I wrote *And Be A Villain* I didn't plan or even consciously contemplate, subsequent appearance or appearances of Zeck" (sic; McAleer/Little, Brown, p. 564). This assertion seems improbable, but Zeck does prove to be far more ominous as a disembodied voice in *In the Best Families* than as an actual character in the third novel.

The radio show provides a neat but rather unrealized setting for the action. Motives and means are inadequately accounted for, but Wolfe's interrogations and analyses are presented effectively.

17. "Help Wanted, Male"
in *Trouble in Triplicate* (1949)

Victims: Ben Jensen—publisher and politician; shot. Doyle—Jensen's bodyguard; shot.

Client: Wolfe, who has also received a death threat.

Other Principals: Major Emil Jensen—son of Ben. Captain Root—convicted of selling military secrets. Jane Geer—former fiancée of Captain Root. H. H. Hackett—fat decoy employed by Wolfe.

Synopsis: Jensen, who helped Wolfe convict Captain Root, consults Wolfe regarding a death threat. Wolfe refuses to undertake the impossible task of protecting Jensen. The next day, Jensen and his bodyguard are shot. Wolfe advertises for a decoy for himself, and hires H. H. Hackett. As Archie prepares to bring Emil Jensen and Jane Geer into the office to meet Hackett-Wolfe, he hears a shot and finds the decoy wounded in the ear. Wolfe, sitting at his spy hole, happened not to see who fired the shot and Emil and Jane happened to be observing one another at that moment. Wolfe detects a clue and deduces a murderer.

Comment: At least three extremely improbable coincidences (two involving the three unseeing witnesses) mar an ingenious plot. World War II provides the background to this story (first published several years before being collected in book form). Panzer, Durkin, Cather, and Keems are fighting overseas, and Archie tries vainly to obtain an assignment in Germany. Although Stout inserted explicit statements of his patriotic sentiments in the Wolfe series, he never indulged in political melodramas involving sinister Nazis and elaborate conspiracies.

18. "Instead of Evidence"
in *Trouble in Triplicate* (1949)

Victims: Eugene Poor—partner in a prosperous novelty firm; exploding cigar. Arthur Howell—employee in a munitions firm; automobile accident.

Client: Eugene Poor.

Other Principals: Martha Poor—wife of Eugene. Conroy Blaney—eccentric inventor and partner of Eugene. Helen Vardis—employee at Blaney and Poor. Joe Groll—employee at Blaney and Poor.

Synopsis: Convinced that his partner, Conroy Blaney, is going to murder him, Eugene Poor hires Wolfe to avenge his anticipated death. He dies the same evening while smoking a cigar loaded with a secret new explosive. Wolfe discovers a connection with an unsolved murder. He convinces the murderer that escape is impossible, then allows the murderer to commit suicide.

Comment: The plot involves an unusual twist to a familiar detective story device.

19. "Before I Die"
in *Trouble in Triplicate* (1949)

Victims: Angelina Murphy—Dazy Perrit's decoy daughter; shot. Dazy Perrit—gangster and black marketeer; shot.

Client: Dazy Perrit.

Other Principals: Beulah Page—Dazy's actual daughter. Morton Shane—Beulah's fiancé. Thumbs Meeker and Fabian—prominent gangsters.

Synopsis: In order to protect his daughter, Dazy Perrit has employed Angelina Murphy to act as a decoy. Angelina has begun to blackmail him, and he comes to Wolfe to seek assistance in controlling her. Angelina and then Perrit and his bodyguard are gunned down from passing cars. Wolfe gathers the principals in his office and exposes the murderer, who is killed while attempting to shoot Wolfe.

Comment: Wolfe contrives to execute justice. The murderer's indictment and trial might cause an emotional strain on an innocent person. Therefore, Wolfe sets up the situation resulting in the justifiable homicide. Wolfe's aside regarding lawyers—"They are inveterate hedgers. They think everything has two sides, which is nonsense"—points to a basic appeal of the detective genre: its commitment to a clearcut morality in which evil-doing is inexcusable and retribution is unapologetic. Wolfe also argues that the wishes of gangsters are as much entitled to respect as are those of "an oil marauder or a steel bandit."

20. *The Second Confession* (1949)

Victim: Louis Rony—lawyer and agent of Arnold Zeck; automobile accident.

Clients: James U. Sperling—Chairman of the Board, Continental Mines Corporation. Arnold Zeck—criminal mastermind.

Other Principals: Gwenn Sperling—daughter of James U. and infatuated with Louis Rony. Mrs. Sperling, James U. Sperling, Jr., Madeline Sperling—wife, son, and eldest daughter of James U. Paul Emerson—radio news commentator. Webster Kane—economist employed by James U.

Synopsis: Sperling hires Wolfe to prove that Rony is a Communist, this to disabuse the infatuated Gwenn. Wolfe agrees at least to investigate Rony. Zeck demands that Wolfe give up the investigation and enforces the demand by having his agents machine gun Wolfe's rooftop greenhouse. Wolfe defiantly decides to travel to Sperling's upstate estate to pursue the inquiry. While he is there Rony is murdered. Sperling extends Wolfe's commission to include the murder. Webster Kane confesses to the crime, claiming it was accidental. Unsatisfied, Wolfe persists, and Zeck pays him $50,000 to continue. Wolfe discovers that one of the principals is indeed a Communist. He gathers everyone in his office and exposes the Communist killer.

Comment: Zeck remains disembodied, but his character is further defined. Wolfe: "He has varied and extensive sources of income. All of them are illegal and some of them are morally repulsive. Narcotics, smuggling, industrial and commercial rackets, gambling, waterfront blackguardism, professional larceny, blackmailing, political malfeasance—that by no means exhausts his curriculum, but it sufficiently indicates its character." Wolfe accepts Zeck's $50,000 with the expectation of eventually using it in a campaign to destroy Zeck.

Wolfe apparently maintains an informer inside the American Communist Party. He uses his source to publish an account of the Communist conspiracy to assist the Presidential candidacy of Henry Wallace (1948), and he extorts the cooperation of two prominent members of the party. They identify and shun the homicidal party member. Wolfe and Archie both despise the Communists; Wolfe actively supports the World Federalists (Stout himself was a founding member of the United World Federalists). As part of his compensation from Sperling, Wolfe demands that he cease to sponsor the anti-World Federalist (and anti-Wolfe) commentator, Emerson.

21. "Man Alive"
in *Three Doors to Death* (1950)

Victims: Paul Nieder—partner in Daumery and Nieder, New York couturiers; suicide (geysered to death in Yellowstone Park). Jean Daumery—partner in Daumery and Nieder; suicide (drowned). Helen Daumery wife of Jean; beloved of Paul; suicide (horseback riding accident).

Client: Cynthia Nieder—fashion designer, model, and niece and heir of Paul.

Other Principals: Bernard Daumery—nephew and heir of Jean. Henry R. Demarest—Daumery family lawyer. Ward Roper—designer for Daumery and Nieder. Polly Zarella—production manager for Daumery and Nieder.

Synopsis: Cynthia Nieder consults Wolfe after she recognizes her "dead" uncle in the audience at a fashion show. A few days later, the battered body of her disguised uncle is discovered in the offices of Daumery and Nieder. Wolfe forces all of the principals to gather in his office and uses a stratagem to identify the murderer.

Comment: A melodramatic plot, unusual in that most of the principals claim solid alibis. Most suspects in the later Wolfe novels and novellas are conveniently alibiless.

22. "Omit Flowers"
in *Three Doors to Death* (1950)

Victim: Floyd Whitten—second husband of Mrs. Whitten; stabbed.

Client: Virgil Pompa—chef.

Other Principals: Marko Vukcic—Wolfe's friend and Virgil Pompa's advocate. Julie Alving—Floyd Whitten's former flame. Jerome Landy, Mortimer Landy, Phoebe Landy, Eve Landy Bahr, and Daniel Bahr—sons, daughters, and son-in-law of Mrs. Whitten by her first marriage.

Synopsis: H. R. Landy made a fortune through a chain of restaurants—"Ambrosia's"—supervised by Virgil Pompa. Following Landy's death, his widow, Mrs. Whitten, intended to install her second husband as head of the corporation. She quarrels with Pompa. Whitten's body is discovered in a room to which only the Whitten/Landy family and Pompa had access. The police arrest Pompa, and Marko Vukcic asks Wolfe to intercede on his behalf. Archie does some clever investigating; Mrs. Whitten is assaulted; Wolfe questions the family and, separately, Julie Alving. Finally he gathers all of the principals in his office and exposes the murderer.

Comment: The Ambrosia chain recalls the Pratteria's (*Some Buried Caesar*); Pompa recalls Les Quinze Maîtres (*Too Many Cooks*). The action is neatly plotted; some of the characters are unusual.

23. "Door to Death"
in *Three Doors to Death (1950)*

Victim: Dini Lauer—nurse to Mrs. Pitcairn; fumigated.

Client: Andrew Krasicki—gardener, orchidologist, and Dini Lauer's fiancé.

Other Principals: Mr. and Mrs. Joseph G. Pitcairn—wealthy residents of Westchester County. Donald and Sybil Pitcairn—son and daughter. Neil and Vera Imbrie—Pitcairn butler and cook. Gus Treble—Pitcairn assistant gardener.

Synopsis: Wolfe and Archie drive to the Pitcairn estate to obtain the services of Andrew Krasicki as a temporary replacement for Theodore Horstmann, who is with his dying mother in Ohio. While interviewing Krasicki, they discover the body of Dini Lauer in the greenhouse, poisoned by ciphogene gas. The police arrest Krasicki, and Pitcairn expels Wolfe from his estate. Wolfe, Archie, and Saul Panzer return surreptitiously at night. Wolfe breaks into the house, blackmails the Pitcairns into gathering for an interrogation, and through a stratagem forces a confession from the murderer.

Comment: The action is unexceptional, but it does suggest the lengths to which Wolfe will go to secure the services of a first-class gardener.

24. *In the Best Families* (1950)

Victim: Mrs. Barry Rackham—wealthy but unattractive heiress; stabbed.

Client: Mrs. Barry Rackham.

Other Principals: Barry Rackham—fortune-hunting husband. Calvin Leeds—cousin to and neighbor of Mrs. Rackham. Annabel Frey, Lina Darrow, Dana Hammond, Oliver A. Pierce—houseguests of the Rackham's. Arnold Zeck—criminal mastermind. Max Christy, Pete Roeder—agents of Zeck.

Synopsis: Mrs. Rackham employs Wolfe to investigate her husband's secret source of income. Zeck warns Wolfe not to involve himself in the case. Wolfe involves himself. Archie visits Mrs. Rackham in the country. The evening he arrives, both Mrs. Rackham and her Doberman pinscher are stabbed to death. Upon hearing the news, Wolfe abandons his brownstone. Fritz and Theodore find other jobs; Archie sets himself up as an independent investigator. Several months later, Roeder, acting for Zeck, hires him to follow Rackham. Archie is astonished when Wolfe suddenly returns. Together they choreograph a situation in which the criminal mastermind and his pawns are murdered. Wolfe then gathers the remaining principals in his office and reveals the identity of Mrs. Rackham's killer.

Comment: The third and climactic Zeck novel reveals the inadequacy of Stout's embodiment of Evil. Professor Moriarty was also an elusive personality, but the final debacle with Holmes at Reichenbach Falls suggested a titanic struggle between Good and Evil. Arnold Zeck is, by reputation, at most an oversized gangster; in person he seems merely a gangster—tough-talking, but gullible, vulnerable, and banal. The events that surround his demise are more tawdry than grand. Still, he does provoke Wolfe's dramatic flight and even more dramatic dieting. The reader is more affected by the reactions of the detective than by the actions of the criminal—even those of a criminal mastermind. This suggests both the special strength and the special weakness of the Wolfe series.

The murder of Mrs. Rackham is poorly motivated, but Wolfe's solution of the case is neat. Archie continues his dalliance with Lily Rowan. And there is a sign of changing times when the Rackham house party turns down the lights and devotes itself to watching three television programs. After 1950, it seems, the inquiring detective cannot depend upon an evening of revealing conversation with the upper class.

25. "Bullet for One"
in *Curtains for Three* (1950)

Victim: Sigmund Keyes—"top-drawer industrial designer"; shot.

Clients: Dorothy Keyes—restive daughter of Sigmund. Ferdinand Pohl—dissatisfied financier. Frank Broadyko—competitor. Audrey Rooney—fired secretary. Wayne Safford—stable hand and enamored of Audrey.

Other Principals: Victor Talbot—Keyes's publicity agent and Dorothy's fiancé.

Synopsis: Keyes has been murdered while riding his horse around Central Park. Wolfe's clients (and Victor Talbot as well) all have fair-to-middling motives for killing Keyes and all claim fair-to-middling alibis. Wolfe breaks one alibi and arranges a recreation of the crime which causes the murderer to panic into self-incrimination.

Comment: An extremely artificial story: everyone has a motive; every one has an alibi; at some point everyone is arrested or threatened with arrest (for assault and battery, disturbing the peace, perjury, forgery, receipt of stolen goods); in the end, everyone (with the single necessary exception) is free, happy, and reconciled—a marriage is promised and a person presumed poor proves to be rich. The scene of the crime is fanciful;

Wolfe browbeats Cramer and pointlessly conceals aspects of his investigation from Archie; the criminal's panic is improbable. In short, the plot virtually parodies the conventions of the Nero Wolfe tale.

26. "The Gun with Wings"
in *Curtains for Three* (1950)

Victim: Alberto Mion—opera tenor; shot.

Clients: Peggy Mion—wife of Alberto. Frederick Weppler—music critic.

Other Principals: Clara James—rumored to have been seduced by Mion. Clifford James—opera tenor and father of Clara. Dr. Nicholas Lloyd—Mion's physician.

Synopsis: Peggy Mion and Frederick Weppler consult Wolfe four months after Mion apparently committed suicide. They are in love, but are troubled by doubts regarding the supposed suicide weapon. Wolfe inquires into the damage done to Mion's throat when he was attacked by Clifford James. He accounts for the mysteries regarding the murder weapon, and then gathers all of the principals in his office where he demonstrates that the death was indeed murder and discloses the identity of the murderer.

Comment: The story is pleasant but uninspired, typical of the standardized Wolfe entertainment.

27. "Disguise for Murder"
in *Curtains for Three* (1950)

Victims: Doris Hatten—a kept woman; strangled. Cynthia Brown—a con woman; strangled.

Client: none.

Other Principals: Colonel Percy Brown—con man, Cynthia's "brother" and accomplice. Mrs. Orwin, Eugene Orwin—mother and son, intended victims of the scam. Homer N. Carlisle and wife—flower fanciers. Malcolm Vedder—flower fancier and psychiatrist.

Synopsis: Wolfe has invited the two hundred odd members of the Manhattan Flower Club to visit his rooftop greenhouse. Cynthia Brown takes Archie aside and confesses her participation in a confidence scam. She declares that she has just recognized the murderer of her former girlfriend, Doris Hatten. During Archie's brief absence from the office, someone strangles Cynthia. Inspector Cramer arrives, questions witnesses, and seals Wolfe's office. Wolfe deduces the identity of the murderer and has Archie send a note requesting a meeting. The murderer calls Archie and arranges the interview. Archie manages to convince the murderer's accomplices to betray their boss.

Comment: The brownstone setting is noteworthy, but the story is otherwise a weak performance. The execution of both murders is highly improbable. Wolfe's stratagem of having Archie arrange an appointment with the criminal (whose identity Archie coyly conceals) seems pointless. It succeeds only because the accomplices allow themselves to be astonished. Finally, the identity of the murderer strains credibility.

28. *Murder by the Book* (1951)

Victims: Joan Wellman—reader for a publishing house; automobile accident. Rachel Abrams—typist; defenestrated. Leonard Dykes—law clerk and would-be novelist; drowned.

Client: John R. Wellman—father of Joan.

Other Principals: Law Firm of Corrigan, Phelps, Kustin & Briggs—Partners: James A. Corrigan, Emmet Phelps, Louis Kustin, Frederick Briggs. Disbarred Partner—Conroy O'Malley. Secretaries—Sue Dondero, Blanche Duke, and eight others. Mrs. Abrams—mother of Rachel. Peggy Potter—sister of Leonard Dykes.

Synopsis: John R. Wellman employs Wolfe to investigate the death of his daughter, which the police have dismissed as a hit-and-run accident. Wolfe connects her death with that of Leonard Dykes through the pen name (Baud Archer) Dykes used when submitting the manuscript of his novel to Joan Wellman's publishing house. Archie, pursuing the manuscript, enters Rachel Abrams's office moments after she has fallen from her seventh-story window. Archie entertains the women of the Corrigan, Phelps firm at dinner and learns the details of Conroy O'Malley's disbarment for jury tampering. Wolfe prepares a trap by sending Archie to Los Angeles, where he arranges for Dykes's sister to claim to possess a copy of her brother's manuscript. Corrigan takes the bait, flies to Los Angeles, returns to New York, and then apparently commits suicide, having first mailed an unsigned confession to Wolfe. Wolfe gathers the principals in his office, reconstructs the true sequence of events, and identifies the murderer.

Comment: A well-plotted novel, despite the needless coincidence of Archie's visit and Rachel's defenestration. The characters are more individual than usual in the later novels—the grieving parents, especially the decent Peoria businessman, John R. Wellman, and the admirably sensible sister, Mrs. Potter. Archie demonstrates his mastery at his dinner party for the secretaries, and Wolfe's three gatherings with the law partners are functional. Stout has even taken the trouble to individualize the partners.

Corrigan dies while "The Life of Riley" plays on the radio in the background; a janitor expresses some doubts as to whether the "wonder boy," Mickey Mantle, will live up to expectations.

29. "The Cop-Killer"
in *Triple Jeopardy* (1952)

Victim: Jake Wallen—policeman; stabbed.

Clients: Carl and Tina Vardas—employees of the Goldenrod Barber Shop.

Other Principals: Joel Fickler, Ed Graboff, Philip Toracco, Tom Yerkes, Jimmie Kirk, Janet Stahl—barbers and manicurists at the Goldenrod Barber Shop.

Synopsis: Carl and Tina Vardas, refugees from Stalin's Russia and illegal immigrants in America, flee to Archie after Wallen questions them regarding a hit-and-run accident. Archie visits the Goldenrod, his regular barber shop, and discovers that Wallen was murdered in the shop at about the time the Vardases fled. Wolfe reluctantly takes up the case and proceeds to the Goldenrod. He examines the principals and discovers the identity of the murderer.

Comment: Janet Stahl, an aspiring actress and an ambitious liar, supplies the story with an entertaining diversion. Archie and Wolfe split hairs to maintain their technical innocence while harboring the fugitives.

30. "The Squirt and the Monkey"
in *Triple Jeopardy* (1952)

Victim: Adrian Getz—the squirt and a friend of Harry Koven; shot.

Client: Harry Koven—author of the comic strip, *Dazzle Dan*.

Other Principals: Marcelle Koven—wife of Harry. Patricia Lowell—

Koven's agent. Pete Jordan—artist working for Koven. Byram Hildrebrand—artist working for Koven.

Synopsis: Harry Koven hires Archie to investigate a missing gun. While Archie is at Koven's house, Adrian Getz is murdered with Archie's gun. When Koven denies hiring Archie, Inspector Cramer arrests Archie and threatens Wolfe with the loss of his license. Wolfe threatens Koven with a million-dollar lawsuit to force him to gather the principals in Wolfe's office. Wolfe exposes the killer.

Comment: The plot seems incoherent: there is no reason for the crime to have occurred when and how it did, and the motive-mongering is silly. A monkey plays a minor role in the crime. Wolfe's solution depends in part upon his reading of a rather obvious allegory inserted annually in the *Dazzle Dan* strip.

31. "Home to Roost"
in *Triple Jeopardy* (1952)

Victim: Arthur Rackell—member of the U.S. Communist Party; poisoned.

Clients: Benjamin Rackell—wealthy importer and uncle of Arthur. Pauline Rackell—domineering wife of Benjamin.

Other Principals: Ormond Leddegard—labor-management mediator. Fifi Goheen—former Debutante of the Year. Della Devlin—novelties buyer. Henry Jameson Heath—wealthy contributor to Communist causes. Carol Berk—"TV contact specialist."

Synopsis: Arthur Rackell is poisoned at a dinner party shortly after confessing to his aunt that his membership in the Communist Party has been part of an FBI undercover operation. His uncle and aunt employ Wolfe to investigate the murder. They gather the dinner party guests in Wolfe's office. A variety of motives emerges. Wolfe decides upon a stratagem which requires him to seem to suborn perjury. The device works; the Communist Party repudiates the secret member who proves to be a murderer.

Comment: The story's original title, "Nero Wolfe and the Communist Killer," supplies the appropriate emphasis. Wolfe again disparages the party, expressing the "odium" in which he holds it. Nonetheless, he also rejects Red-baiting: "I deplore the current tendency to accuse people of pro-communism irresponsibly and unjustly." As in *The Second Confession*, the party is quick to disown an errant member, but Party membership functions as a primary motive for the crime. Wolfe bulldozes the FBI with the same smugness as he bulldozes the city police.

32. *Prisoner's Base* (1952) ♌

Victims: Priscilla Eads—heiress to the Softdown textile fortune; strangled. Margaret Fomos—Priscilla's maid; strangled.

Client: Archie Goodwin.

Other Principals: Sarah Jaffe—friend of Priscilla. Eric Hagh—Priscilla's ex-husband. Andreas Fomos—Margaret's husband. Jay Luther Brucker—President of Softdown. Bernard Quest—Vice-President of Softdown. Oliver Pitkin—Secretary and Treasurer of Softdown. Viola Duday—Assistant Secretary of Softdown. Perry Helmar—legal counsel to Softdown.

Synopsis: Priscilla Eads seeks refuge in Wolfe's house, but refuses to discuss the nature of the threat to her safety. Archie admits her; Wolfe dismisses her; that night she and her maid are strangled. Archie reacts emotionally, and undertakes an investigation independent of Wolfe. He is arrested for impersonating a police officer, and Wolfe, in the process of obtaining his release, claims Archie as his client. The fortune Priscilla would have inherited is now to be distributed to five Softdown executives. Priscilla's former husband arrives from Venezuela with a claim to one half of the inheritance. Wolfe gathers the principals in his office for a lengthy interrogation. The same night another murder is committed, intensifying Archie's personal interest in the case. The authorities ask Wolfe to direct a re-enactment of the office gathering. He consents, but before the recreation can begin, he exposes the criminal.

Comment: Strong characterization compensates for a weak plot. The women—Priscilla, Sarah, and Viola—are attractive, and Oliver Pitkin has a fine moment at the first gathering. (The gathering itself, occupying two chapters, represents one of Wolfe's better performances.) Archie's personal involvements add color to the narrative. His act of violence at the revelation of the culprit is particularly interesting.

33. *The Golden Spiders* (1953)   8

Victims: Pete Drossos—a street-wise twelve-year-old; automobile accident. Laura Fromm—wealthy widow and philanthropist; automobile accident.

Matthew Birch—special agent of the Immigration and Naturalization Service; automobile accident.

Clients: Pete Drossos. Laura Fromm.

Other Principals: Angela Wright—Executive Secretary of the Association for the Aid of Displaced Persons (Assadip). Dennis Horan—lawyer for Assadip. Jean Estey—secretary to Laura Fromm. James Albert Maddox—lawyer for the Fromm estate. Paul Kuffner—public relations expert serving Assadip. Vincent Lipscomb—magazine publisher. Lawrence "Lips" Egan—minor gangster.

Synopsis: While working the "wipe racket" on cars waiting for a traffic light to change, Pete Drossos sees a woman mouth a plea to call the police. Pete prefers to consult Wolfe. When Pete is killed the following day, the police connect his death with that of the Immigration Service agent, Matthew Birch. Wolfe involves himself in the affair, publishing a notice which brings Laura Fromm to his office. She offers him a retainer, but before she can return to declare her suspicions, she too is murdered. Wolfe devises a stratagem for Archie to execute and also mobilizes Saul, Fred, and Orrie. He uncovers a conspiracy to blackmail illegal immigrants. Finally, he gathers the principals in his office and identifies the murderer.

Comment: The principals are very lightly sketched. Lips Egan does provide the occasion for some hardboiled action, and Wolfe does do some effective thinking. There are incidental references to the Korean War and to the McCarthy hearings (Archie: "If you were a United States Senator, naturally I wouldn't expect you to name my accuser, but since you're not, go climb a tree"). Orrie Cather's first name is Orvald.

34. "This Won't Kill You"
in *Three Men Out* (1954)

Victim: Nick Ferrone—New York Giants second baseman; beaten.

Client: Emil Chisholm—part-owner of the Giants.

Other Principals: Lew Baker, Con Prentiss, Joe Eston, Nat Neill—respectively the catcher, shortstop, third baseman, and center fielder of the Giants. Art Kinney—Giants manager. Bill Moyse—back-up catcher. Lila Moyse—wife of Bill. Dan Gale—uncle of Lila Moyse. Beaky Durkin—Giants scout and Ferrone's discoverer.

Synopsis: Wolfe and Archie escort a guest, Pierre Mondor (*Too Many Cooks*), to the seventh game of the World Series between New York and Boston. The Red Sox win, 15-2. Four Giants players—Baker, Prentiss, Eston, and Neill—were drugged prior to the game. Chisholm employs Wolfe to investigate the incident. Archie discovers the body of Ferrone in the Giants' locker room, and later learns that Dan Gale had attempted to fix the game. Wolfe gathers the principals in the owner's office and exposes the murderer.

Comment: The scene is remarkable; Wolfe never leaves the Polo Grounds. Wolfe and Archie each make crucial observations regarding the reactions of individuals to the outcome of the game, and as a result can both claim to have solved the crime.

35. "Invitation to Murder"
in *Three Men Out* (1954)

Victim: Herman Lewent—a drone and brother of the heiress, Beryl Huck; beaten.

Client: Herman Lewent.

Other Principals: Theodore Huck—infirm widower and heir of his deceased wife, Beryl Huck. Cassie O'Shea, Sylvia Marcy, Dorothy Riff—respectively, Huck's housekeeper, nurse, and secretary. Paul Thayer—nephew of Theodore Huck.

Synopsis: In order to insure the continuance of a stipend from his father's estate, Herman Lewent wishes to know which of the three women in Huck's household his brother-in-law intends to marry (and thus into whose graces he should insinuate himself). Archie questions the various prospects, but before reaching any conclusions, discovers that his client has been murdered. He tricks Wolfe into making an excursion to Huck's house, and Wolfe, through stratagem and observation, discovers the culprit.

Comment: Aside from the rather preposterous original commission, the story is unexceptional.

36. "The Zero Clue"
in *Three Men Out* (1954)

Victim: Leo Heller—probability expert; beaten.

Client: Leo Heller.

Other Principals: Agatha Abbey—magazine editor. Susan Mature—nurse. Mrs. Albert Tillotson—society matron. Jack Ennis—inventor. Karl Busch—no visible means of support. John R. Winslow—prospective heir, all clients of Leo Heller.

Synopsis: Heller, a former mathematics professor who claims probability theory as his medium of clairvoyance, arranges an appointment with Archie to discuss one of the clients of his service. Archie arrives to discover Heller's body, and the six clients visiting his office that day become the prime suspects. Heller left an enigmatic clue on his desk in the form of an arrangement of pencils which suggests to Inspector Cramer the initials "NW" and to Wolfe the number six. The number six happens to figure in the case histories of each of the clients, but Wolfe suddenly reinterprets the clue, gathers the six clients in his office, and exposes the murderer.

Comment: The generic cliché of the baffling dying message props up an extremely artificial plot, with an abundance of coincidental sixes and an allusion to Mesopotamian mathematics.

37. *The Black Mountain* (1954)

Victims: Marko Vukcic—owner of Rusterman's Restaurant, Wolfe's oldest friend; shot. Carla (Mrs. William R.) Britton—Wolfe's adopted daughter; tortured and shot.

Client: none.

Other Principals: Danilo Vukcic—Marko's nephew; triple agent: Yugoslavian, Albanian (Russian), and Spirit of the Black Mountain (resistance). Peter Zov—double agent: Yugoslavian, Russian. Gospo Stritar—head of Secret Police, Titograd, Yugoslavia. Josip Pasic, Stan Kosor—Spirit of the Black Mountain.

Synopsis: Vukcic, who has appeared intermittently throughout the series as Wolfe's closest friend, is gunned down in front of his apartment. Convinced that the motive for the killing was Vukcic's support for an underground anti-Tito movement, the Spirit of the Black Mountain, Wolfe's adopted daughter, Carla, travels to Montenegro to investigate. Before she is caught and killed, she sends Wolfe a message indicating that the killer has returned to Montenegro. Wolfe and Archie fly to Bari, Italy, via London and Rome. They enter Yugoslavia covertly by sea. They proceed to Titograd, where Wolfe marches into the office of Gospo Stritar and proclaims that he (as "Tone Stara") and his son ("Alex") have returned to their homeland without papers in order to decide for themselves which political faction to support with the fortune they have accumulated in America—Tito's regime, the Russian puppets in Albania, or the Spirit of the Black Mountain. Stritar permits them to make further inquiries. By contacting Danilo Vukcic, Wolfe and Archie manage to visit a secret camp of the resistance movement. They cross the border into Albania, kill a Russian agent and two Albanian subordinates, and rescue Peter Zov, one of Stritar's men. They then return covertly to Italy. Wolfe and Archie board the same ship as does Vukcic's assassin, and as they enter New York harbor, Wolfe exposes the killer (and receives a flesh wound in the leg).

Comment: The deaths of Vukcic and Carla seem wasted in a somewhat farcical melodrama that has the normally immobile detective suddenly flying around the world and hiking across countrysides and up and down mountains. The secret police are ridiculously incompetent, and the mechanism of coincidence is much abused. There is perhaps some interest in the moment when Wolfe and Archie pass by the stone house in which Wolfe was born, but it remains only a vague shape in the night.

Wolfe declares to Carla the necessity of supporting the cause of human freedom, but he dismisses the Spirit of the Black Mountain as "naive." Wolfe also reaffirms an important ethical standard by refusing to kill Marko's assassin when the occasion offers itself: "If personal vengeance were the only factor I could . . . go and stick a knife in him and finish it, but that would be accepting the intolerable doctrine that man's sole responsibility is to his own ego. That was the doctrine of Hitler, as it is now of Malenkov and Tito and Franco and Senator McCarthy; masquerading as the basis of freedom, it is the oldest and toughest of the enemies of freedom." And so the improbable business of arranging to return to New York in such a way as to be able to subject the assassin to due process has this significant ideological foundation. Wolfe thus distinguishes his practice from that of the then most recent and most sensational addition to the corps of New York City detectives, the notoriously unscrupulous Mike Hammer.

38. *Before Midnight* (1955)

Victim: Louis Dahlmann—advertising executive; shot.

Clients: The advertising firm of Lippert, Buff and Assa (Partners: Oliver Buff, Vernon Assa, Patrick O'Garro).

Other Principals: Rudolf Hanson—attorney for Lippert, Buff and Assa. Talbot Heery—head of Heery Products, a major cosmetics company. Susan Tescher, Philip Younger, Carol Wheelock, Gertrude Frazee, Harold Rollins—Pour Amour contest finalists.

Synopsis: Louis Dahlmann conceives the stunt of advertising Pour Amour perfume by conducting a contest which requires entrants to solve a series of rhymed puzzles. Dahlmann is found murdered and his copy of the solutions to the puzzles is missing. The advertising firm employs Wolfe in order to relieve its embarrassment regarding the damaged integrity of the contest. Wolfe eventually gathers all of the principals in his office, but before he can explore his case, one of the principals is poisoned, thus aborting the session. Humiliated by this challenge to his authority, Wolfe fully commits himself to the murder investigation. In pursuit of his inquiry he travels to the offices of Lippert, Buff and Assa, and there he discovers incriminating evidence and identifies the murderer.

Comment: The novel suffers in the comparison it begs with Dorothy Sayers' *Murder Must Advertise*. Stout makes no attempt to reproduce the environment of a functioning agency, and the logic of his plot is very weak (though Wolfe does use a certain device effectively). The winner of the Pour Amour contest is never announced.

39. "When a Man Murders. . ."
in *Three Witnesses* (1956)

Victim: Sidney Karnow—millionaire; reported killed in Korea; shot.

Clients: Caroline Karnow Aubry—widow of Sidney; wife of Paul Aubry. Paul Aubry—car salesman and second husband of Caroline.

Other Principals: Mrs. Raymond Savage—aunt of Sidney Karnow. Richard Savage, Ann Savage Home, Norman Home—respectively, son, daughter, and son-in-law of Mrs. Savage. Jim Beebe—Sidney Karnow's lawyer.

Synopsis: Caroline and Paul Aubry consult Wolfe regarding the problem posed by the news that Sidney Karnow has survived the war in a prisoner-of-war camp and that he has just returned to New York. Archie agrees to speak to Karnow, but discovers him dead in his hotel room. The police arrest Aubry, and Caroline employs Wolfe to exculpate him. Wolfe extorts Inspector Cramer's cooperation in gathering all of the principals in his office. Then, by deducing Karnow's testamentary intentions, Wolfe exposes the murderer.

Comment: Paul and Caroline Aubry happen to have been in Karnow's hotel at the time he was murdered, and not one of the other principals was verifiably otherwise engaged. Wolfe: "How many of the others—Mrs. Savage, her son, Mr. and Mrs. Horne, Mr. Beebe—have been eliminated by alibis?" Inspector Cramer: "Crossed off, no one." Unlimited suspectability is much more convenient than probable. This becomes the standard situation: all of the principals can be charged with a motive of some sort; none of the principals engage in extraneous activities which might interfere with their opportunity to commit the crime.

40. "Die Like a Dog"
in *Three Witnesses* (1956) 4

Victim: Philip Krapf—writer; strangled.

Client: none.

Other Principals: Residents of 29 Arbor Street: Jerome Aland—nightclub performer. Ross Chaffee—painter. Richard Meegan—photographer. Victor Talento—lawyer. Jewel Jones—singer; former resident of 29 Arbor Street. Jet (née Bootsy)—black Labrador Retriever.

Synopsis: Archie walks to Arbor Street, intending to return a raincoat left behind by a rejected client. Recognizing the homicide squad outside the entrance, he passes by the address, but he is followed home to Wolfe's brownstone by a dog which proves to have belonged to Philip Krapf, the murder victim. Wolfe decides to inject himself in the case. He locates Jewel Jones, who has had a variety of relationships with the principals: wife, mistress, model, friend. Wolfe gathers all of the principals in his office and exposes the murderer.

Comment: The Lab provides the main attraction of the story: he occasions some amusing byplay between Archie and Wolfe, and he provokes a crucial deduction. In the end he seems to be adopted into Wolfe's household, though, like Dr. Watson's bull pup, he is never heard of again.

41. "The Next Witness" 4
in *Three Witnesses* (1956)

Victim: Marie Willis—operator in Bagby's answering service; strangled.

Client: Leonard Ashe—theatrical producer.

Other Principals: Clyde Bagby—head of Bagby Answers, Inc. Helen Weltz—operator for Bagby Answers, Inc. Robina Keane—movie actress; wife of Leonard Ashe.

Synopsis: Because Leonard Ashe had attempted to employ Wolfe to pay Marie Willis to eavesdrop on the conversations of his wife, Wolfe has been subpoenaed by the prosecution in Ashe's trial for the murder of Marie. Listening to the testimony, Wolfe decides that justice is being miscarried, and he risks prosecution himself by leaving the courtroom and carrying out a quick investigation of Bagby Answers, Inc. He returns to court the following morning and evades a contempt citation by cleverly injecting into his testimony his conclusions regarding the true criminal. Ashe, in gratitude, remunerates him handsomely.

Comment: Wolfe's contempt of court does exact a penalty: he misses his daily routines and is even forced to spend the night concealed in Saul Panzer's apartment. The motive for the crime involves a fairly obvious blackmail scheme.

42. *Might As Well Be Dead* (1956)

Victims: Michael M. Molloy—real estate broker; shot. John Joseph Keems—one of Wolfe's irregular agents; automobile accident. Ella Reyes—maid; beaten.

Client: James R. Herold—owner of the Herold Hardware Company, Omaha, Nebraska.

Other Principals: Paul Herold (aka Peter Hayes)—son of James R. and convicted of the murder of Molloy. Selma Molloy—wife of Michael M. and friend of Peter Hayes. Thomas L. and Fanny Irwin—friends of the Molloys. Jerry and Rita Arkoff—friends of the Molloys. Patrick A.

Degan—friend of the Molloys. Delia Brandt—Michael Molloy's secretary. William Lesser—Delia Brandt's fiancé.

Synopsis: James Herold employs Wolfe to locate the son he had unjustifiably disowned eleven years ago. Archie identifies the son as Peter Hayes, recently convicted of homicide. Archie and Wolfe become convinced of Hayes' innocence. Selma Molloy assists them in their investigation of the case. Wolfe questions the principals, then deploys his agents to pursue further inquiries. While on assignment, Johnny Keems is killed. The Irwins' maid, whom Keems had questioned, is also killed. Finally, yet another of the principals is killed, but Wolfe obtains information which reveals the source of the three hundred thousand dollars found in Molloy's safety deposit box. Wolfe gathers the principals in his office, and in the presence of Inspector Cramer, exposes the murderer.

Comment: The action is unusually sanguine, and the most notable victim is Johnny Keems, who debuted in the series in 1937 and who had appeared intermittently since. He is—or was—the irregular agent who fancied himself Archie's heir apparent. His demise, like that of Marko Vukcic in *The Black Mountain*, seems somewhat wasted. Not until the final Wolfe novel, *A Family Affair*, does Stout fully exploit the advantage of the reader's established interest in the unfortunate fate of one of the series characters.

The abundance of deaths suggests that the murderer is a maniac. A plausible motive for the initial crime is introduced incidentally and late. Wolfe has the decency to share his substantial fee with the widow of Johnny Keems and the mother of Ella Reyes.

43. "Immune to Murder"
in *Three for the Chair* (1957)

Victim: David M. Leeson—Assistant Secretary of State; bludgeoned.

Client: none.

Other Principals: Sally Leeson—wife of David M. O. V. Bragan, head of Hemisphere Oil Company. James Arthur Ferris—head of the Universal Syndicate. Theodore Kelefy—"a new ambassador from a foreign country." Adria Kelefy—wife of Theodore. Spiros Papps—friend of Ambassador Kelefy.

Synopsis: Oil tycoon Bragan has invited Ambassador Kelefy to go trout fishing at his upstate lodge. Both Bragan and Ferris, his competitor and guest, seek a lucrative oil contract with the ambassador's country. Kelefy, having heard of Wolfe's reputation as a gourmet, asks that Wolfe be invited to cook the trout. At the insistence of Secretary Leeson, Wolfe agrees. On the morning of the fishing expedition, Archie discovers Leeson's battered body by the river. Wolfe declines to investigate on behalf of Bragan, but finally—to avoid inconvenience and to repay an affront—he consents to identify the murderer. He insists upon doing so while on the phone to the secretary of state and in the presence of the gathered principals.

Comment: The situation is preposterous: vaguely Middle Eastern ambassadors who whimsically require a famous detective to cook their trout occupy a different level of reality from that which Archie and Wolfe usually inhabit.

44. "A Window for Death"
in *Three for the Chair* (1957)

Victim: Bertram Fyfe—successful uranium prospector; pneumonia.

Client: David Fyfe—high school English teacher; brother of Bertram.

Other Principals: Paul Fyfe—brother of Bertram. Vincent and Louise Tuttle—brother-in-law and sister of Bertram. Johnny Arrow—Bertram's prospecting partner. Frederick Buhl—Fyfe family physician. Anne Goren—nurse.

Synopsis: David Fyfe employs Wolfe to investigate the death of his brother, who has just returned to the city. Although Dr. Buhl has confidently certified pneumonia as the cause of death, David insists upon an unnatural cause. His father had also died of pneumonia in suspicious circumstances. Wolfe questions all of the principals and then pursues a particular line of inquiry. He gathers the principals in his office and discloses the method of the murderer. He then sends a message to Inspector Cramer, identifying the culprit.

Comment: An unexceptional novella.

45. "Too Many Detectives"
in *Three for the Chair* (1957)

Victim: William A. Donahue—instigator of illegal wiretaps; strangled.

Client: none.

Other Principals: Dol Bonner, Sally Colt, Jay Kerr, Steve Amsel, Harland Ide—New York City private investigators.

Synopsis: Albert Hyatt, special deputy of the secretary of state, has summoned a group of detectives to Albany in order to conduct an investigation into illegal wiretapping. Wolfe and Archie had been duped by Donahue into briefly conducting such a wiretap. Hyatt proposes to confront them with Donahue, but finds his star witness dead in the next room. He orders the arrest of Wolfe and Archie, and they are detained as material witnesses until their lawyer posts bail. Wolfe summons the other detectives to his room and discovers that all had been similarly employed by Donahue and that the object of all the wiretaps had been the same. Under Wolfe's supervision, each of the detectives deploys his operatives to pursue the investigation. Wolfe then gathers the principals and the authorities in his hotel room and reveals the identity of the murderer.

Comment: Wolfe is actually incarcerated briefly. The motive of the murderer is distinctive; the plot is entertaining.

46. *If Death Ever Slept* (1957)

Victim: James L. Eber—former secretary of Otis Jarrell; shot.

Client: Otis Jarrell—wealthy capitalist.

Other Principals: Trella Jarrell—wife of Otis. Lois Jarrell—daughter of Otis by his first wife. Wyman Jarrell—son of Otis by his first wife. Susan Jarrell—hypnotically attractive wife of Wyman. Roger Foot—brother of Trella; gambler; permanent house guest. Nora Kent Jarrell's stenographer. Corey Brigham—friend of the Jarrells; Jarrell's business competitor.

Synopsis: Archie and Wolfe squabble over Archie's relationship with Lily Rowan. As a result of their mutual stubbornness, they agree to undertake a commission from Otis Jarrell. Under the pseudonym of Alan Green, Archie enters the Jarrell household, ostensibly to replace Eber, the dismissed secretary, but actually to discover the source of an information leak which is plaguing Jarrell. While Archie is staying in the house, Jarrell discovers that his pistol has been stolen, then Eber's body is discovered. Wolfe gathers the principals in his office, but discovers nothing. A second principal is murdered, and Wolfe again convenes the survivors. Again failing to satisfy himself, Wolfe returns his retainer to Jarrell. He obtains from the police an exhaustive timetable of all alibis and he assigns his own agents to make inquiries. Wolfe finally forces Cramer to gather the principals a third time in his office and there he discloses the identity of the murderer.

Comment: Despite the reproduction of timetables, the plot does not really constitute a fair puzzle. No one has a satisfactory alibi (there is, at least, no wanton motive-mongering). Yet the characters are distinctive enough to make the Jarrell household an interesting one. Susan, the femme fatale, is especially striking. And Orrie Cather's brief performance as "Archie Goodwin" is amusing.

In addition to his usual irregulars (Panzer, Cather, and Durkin), Wolfe resorts to Dol Bonner, the female detective. Lon Cohen, the *Gazette* reporter who has emerged as a convenient and unfailing source of information, again supplies the necessary background data. Eisenhower's budget, the prospects of the Giants moving to San Francisco, Billy Graham, and Jackie Gleason are all mentioned in passing.

Wolfe withholds knowledge of the missing pistol until late in the action. Inspector Cramer is understandably outraged. Archie reports that Wolfe regards as moot the question of whether the second murder might have been avoided had he been more forthcoming.

47. "Christmas Party" 3
in *And Four to Go* (1958)

Victim: Kurt Bottweill—interior decorator; poisoned.

Client: Cherry Quon—Bottweill's attractive receptionist.

Other Principals: Margot Dickey—Bottweill's attractive assistant. Alfred Kiernan—Bottweill's assistant. Emil Hatch—chief of Bottweill's workshop. Mrs. Perry Porter Jeroma—Bottweill's financial backer. Leo Jerome—son of Mrs. Jerome. Santa Claus.

Synopsis: The three women expect a marriage proposal from Bottweill. Margot Dickey attempts to force the issue by arranging for a fake marriage license with Archie. Before she can make her announcement at the office Christmas party, Bottweill dies of cyanide poisoning. The unidentified bartender in a Santa Claus costume flees the scene. Cherry Quon blackmails Wolfe into undertaking an investigation of the crime. He gathers the principals in his office and employs a stratagem to discover the killer.

Comment: Archie's ersatz engagement occasions an interesting sidelight on his relationship with Wolfe, but the story has little else to recommend it. The device through which Wolfe catches his criminal is a trite one. The story contains the last reference to the old irregular, Bill Gore.

48. "Easter Parade"
in *And Four to Go* (1958)

Victim: Mrs. Millard Bynoe—Easter parader; poisoned.

Client: Millard Bynoe—rich philanthropist and orchid fancier.

Other Principals: Tabby—pickpocket in Wolfe's employ. Henry Frimm—executive secretary of a Bynoe philanthropy. Iris Innes—professional photographer; Frimm's former fiancée. Joseph Herrick, Alan Geiss; Augustus Pizzi—freelance photographers.

Synopsis: Wolfe covets a unique new color of orchid which has been cultivated by Millard Bynoe. Mrs. Bynoe will be wearing a blossom in the Easter Parade, and Wolfe assigns Archie to photograph the specimen and Tabby to steal it. Tabby accomplishes the theft just as Mrs. Bynoe collapses on Fifty-fourth Street and dies of strychnine poisoning. The police theorize that a poisoned needle was fired from a camera. Mr. Bynoe arranges a gathering of all the principals at Wolfe's office, and after viewing the slides which Archie took at the Parade, Wolfe identifies the murderer.

Comment: The weapon and the scene are improbable; none of the characters is adequately developed; Wolfe's speculative motive-mongering is unconvincing. Even Stout's reliable sense of style seems hard-pressed in these artificial novellas. Wolfe's reward—a shoot of the new orchid—provides a nice touch, but it lacks the fitness of similar compensations in "Black Orchids" or *Too Many Cooks.*

49. "Fourth of July Picnic"
in *And Four to Go* (1958)

Victim: Philip Holt—Director of Organization, United Restaurant Workers of America; stabbed.

Client: none.

Other Principals: James Korby—President, URWA. Flora Korby—daughter of James. Paul Rago—sauce chef. H. L. Griffin—food importer. Dick Vetter—television personality.

Synopsis: In return for an end to union pressures on his cook, Fritz Brenner, Wolfe consents to deliver a speech at the URWA Independence Day picnic. Taken ill with a stomach upset, Philip Holt retires to a tent where he is visited consecutively by all the principals. When Wolfe makes his visit, he discovers that Holt is dead, not sleeping. He arranges to gather the principals in his office and he makes inquiries regarding motives. The next day he again gathers the principals, this time in Saul Panzer's apartment, and through a stratagem exposes the murderer.

Comment: Despite some more silly motive-mongering, the case presents several interesting aspects. Wolfe is unaccountably peripatetic (there is no sufficient reason to hold the second gathering at Saul's). Prior to the second gathering, Archie issues a direct challenge to the reader, not to identify the killer, but to anticipate Wolfe's stratagem (which proves to be rather unimaginative). Finally, in an effort to provoke revelations at the first gathering, both Wolfe and Archie volunteer autobiographical sketches; though nonfunctional, these sketches do appeal to any follower of the series.

50. "Murder Is No Joke"
in *And Four To Go* (1958)

Victims: Bianca Voss—blackmailer; strangled. Sarah Yare—former stage actress, apparent suicide; poisoned.

Client: none.

Other Principals: Alec Gallant—exclusive couturier. Flora Gallant—Alec's sister. Carl Drew—Gallant's business manager. Emmy Thorne—in charge of contracts and promotions for Gallant.

Synopsis: Flora Gallant solicits Wolfe's assistance in uncovering the nature of Bianca Voss's hold over her brother. She arranges for Wolfe to speak to Bianca over the telephone; during the conversation, Wolfe and Archie hear Bianca being murdered. Wolfe connects the crime with the coincidental death of Sarah Yare, and when the principals spontaneously call upon him, he is able to expose the murderer.

Comment: That the crimes could be committed or concealed seem equally improbable propositions. See also the expanded version, "Frame-Up for Murder," reprinted in *Death Times Three* (see #73).

51. *Champagne for One* (1958)

Victim: Faith Usher—unwed mother; poisoned.

Client: Edwin Laidlaw—wealthy young publisher.

Other Principals: Louise Grantham Robilotti—widow of millionaire philanthropist, Albert Grantham. Robert Robilotti—second husband of Louise. Cecil and Celia Grantham—son and daughter of Mrs. Robilotti. Helen Yarmis, Ethel Varr, Rose Tuttle—unwed mothers. Paul Shuster—young corporate lawyer. Beverly Kent—young diplomat. Austin "Dinky" Byne—nephew of Albert Grantham.

Synopsis: Mrs. Robilotti pursues her first husband's concern for unwed mothers by hosting an annual dinner for four recent beneficiaries of Mr. Grantham's foundation for unwed mothers. Dinky Byne engages Archie to substitute for him as one of the four male escorts. Faith Usher dies at the celebration. She has frequently threatened to commit suicide, and only Archie's testimony that she could not possibly have slipped the cyanide into her champagne prevents her death from being recorded as such. Edwin Laidlaw secretly employs Wolfe to identify the killer. Wolfe interviews most of the principals and instigates a search for Faith Usher's mother. The search succeeds, and Wolfe learns enough to have Inspector Cramer gather all of the principals in his office and to direct a re-enactment of the crime. The reconstruction reveals the method by which the cyanide was introduced into the proper glass, and a final confrontation exposes the murderer.

Comment: The plot is unusual in its emphasis upon the question: how was the poison directed to its target? The solution is clever. The characters are generally undistinguished, but Mrs. Robilotti is a formidable matron.

52. *Plot It Yourself* (1959)

Victims: Jane Ogilvy, Simon Jacobs, Kenneth Rennert—minor writers who have won lawsuits charging major authors with plagiarism; stabbed.

Client: The Joint Committee on Plagiarism of the National Association of Authors and Dramatists (NAAD) and the Book Publishers of America (BPA).

Other Principals: Philip Harvey, Amy Wynn, Mortimer Oshin—writers and members of NAAD. Gerald Knapp, Reuben Imhof, Thomas Dexter—publishers and members of BPA. Cora Ballard—executive secretary, NAAD. Alice Porter—minor writer who twice accuses a major author of plagiarism.

Synopsis: Alice Porter's second lawsuit, this time against Amy Wynn, represents the fifth instance in a four-year pattern of improbable but successfully prosecuted plagiarism cases. The NAAD/BPA Joint Committee employs Wolfe to investigate the case and to terminate the extortions. Wolfe deduces that a single writer is behind the five lawsuits. He accepts a commission to induce one of the successful plaintiffs to reveal the originator of the conspiracy, but three of the four are dead when Archie locates them. Wolfe concentrates upon investigating (and protecting) the fourth, Alice Porter. He gathers the principals in his office and, through a stratagem, forces a confession from the killer.

Comment: The large cast is relatively undistinguished, with the exception of the murderer, whose interesting response to being exposed occupies several pages. The subject of copyright was very important to Stout, who spent many years working to revise the laws to the advantage of writers.

53. "Poison à la Carte"   5
in *Three at Wolfe's Door* (1960)

Victim: Vincent Pyle—"a Wall Street character and a well-known theatrical angel"; poisoned.

Client: none.

Other Principals: Ten for Aristology—a club of epicures. Helen Iacono, Peggy Choate, Carol Annis, Lucy Morgan, Nora Jaret, and seven others—Hebes (twelve actresses hired to serve as waitresses). Fritz Brenner—Wolfe's cook.

Synopsis: Wolfe and Archie have been invited as guests at an Aristology banquet which Fritz Brenner has agreed to prepare. Vincent Pyle, one of the Aristologues, receives arsenic in his first course. Evidence points to the guilt of one of five waitresses. Wolfe devises a stratagem which prompts the killer to attempt to repeat the crime.

Comment: The story is typical of Stout's weaker efforts. The extraordinary Aristologues are dismissed entirely after a few pages; the waitresses are never individualized; there is absolutely no motive for the killing.

54. "Method Three for Murder"
in *Three at Wolfe's Door* (1960)

Victim: Phoebe Arden—an acquaintance of the other principals; stabbed.

Client: Mira Holt—estranged wife of Waldo Kearns.

Other Principals: Waldo Kearns—painter. Judy Bram—taxi driver and friend of Mira Holt. Mr. and Mrs. Gilbert Irving—friends of the other principals.

Synopsis: Mira Holt discovers the body of Phoebe Arden in the taxicab that she has borrowed from Judy Bram. She drives to Wolfe's residence to seek counsel. The police arrest her for the crime. After pursuing some preliminary inquiries, Wolfe gathers the principals in his office and reveals the identity of the killer.

Comment: The motive for the execution of the crime is weak, but the story opens with a squabble between Archie and Wolfe that leads to a temporary rupture; as a result, Mira is officially Archie's client, not Wolfe's.

55. "The Rodeo Murder"
in *Three at Wolfe's Door* (1960)

Victim: Wade Eisler—"well-known figure in sporting and theatrical circles"; lassoed.

Client: Lily Rowan—Archie's long-standing romantic interest.

Other Principals: Harvey Creve, Cal Barrow, Mel Fox—cowboys. Anna Casado, Nan Karlin, Laura Jay—cowgirls. Roger Dunning—promoter of the World Series Rodeo.

Synopsis: Lily Rowan hosts a party in her tenth-story Park Avenue penthouse. The three cowboys hold a roping contest from the balcony. Later, the body of Eisler, a major backer of the World Series Rodeo and a notorious womanizer, is discovered strangled on the rear terrace. The police hold Cal Barrow and Archie as material witnesses. Lily Rowan calls upon Wolfe to discover the murderer. Wolfe gathers all of the principals in his office and reveals the identity of the killer.

Comment: The attempt to exploit an uncommon scene is more successful than usual. Wolfe's discovery of the killer involves some plausible reasoning, and there is a nicely handled romantic subplot.

56. *Too Many Clients* (1960) 6

Victims: Thomas G. Yeager—Vice-President of Consolidated Plastic Products; shot. Maria Perez—witness to Yeager's love nest; shot.

Clients: Consolidated Plastic Products. Ellen Yeager—wife of Thomas G. Yeager. Cesar and Felita Perez—parents of Maria.

Other Principals: Benedict Aiken—President of Consolidated Plastic Products. Julia McGee—Thomas Yeager's secretary. Meg Duncan—Broadway actress. Austin Hough—Assistant Professor of English. Dinah Hough—Austin Hough's wife.

Synopsis: A man claiming to be Thomas G. Yeager hires Archie to determine whether he is being followed. When "Yeager" fails to make a rendezvous, Archie investigates and discovers that Yeager has been murdered and that the man who engaged him has not been Yeager. Archie also discovers Yeager's love nest in a building maintained for him by the Perezes. Yeager's many mistresses included Julia McGee, Meg Duncan, and Dinah Hough. Maria Perez is murdered, and Archie confirms that she had been blackmailing Yeager. Wolfe decides to share none of these discoveries with the police. He identifies the killer, obtains a holograph confession, and permits a suicide.

Comment: Wolfe's ethics are questionable. He conceals the existence of the love nest and, by insisting only upon a confession of guilt in the murder of Yeager, he insures that the case of Maria Perez will remain officially unsolved. The motive for the murder of Yeager emerges like a *deus ex machina*. Sex becomes an overt theme in this novel: Yeager is a satyr, and a woman attempts to seduce Archie; Austin Hough punishes his wife's infidelities with a severe beating.

57. *The Final Deduction* (1961)

Victims: Dinah Utley—secretary to Althea Vail; automobile accident. Jimmy Vail—second husband of Althea Vail; crushed by a statue of Benjamin Franklin.

Clients: Althea Vail—wealthy widow of Harold F. Tedder and wife of Jimmy. Noel Tedder—son of Althea and Harold F.

Other Principals: Margot Tedder—snobbish daughter of Harold F. and Althea. Andrew Frost—Tedder family lawyer. Ralph Purcell—brother of Althea.

Synopsis: Wolfe agrees to assist Althea Vail in obtaining the safe release of her kidnaped husband, Jimmy. Wolfe infers that Dinah Utley is implicated in the crime. Jimmy is released unharmed, but the same night Dinah Utley is murdered. The next day, Jimmy Vail's body is discovered beneath a statue of Benjamin Franklin in the library of the Vail's Manhattan mansion. Althea promises to give the money paid to her husband's kidnappers ($500,000) to her son Noel, should he be able to recover it. For a twenty percent commission, Wolfe enables Noel to recover the money. Wolfe then invites the murderer to his office and through a reconstruction of events provokes a confession.

Comment: The kidnap plot and the murder plot are equally improbable. Archie's combustible relationship with Wolfe remains entertaining, but relations with the police and the press (Lon Cohen) have become predictable. The Tedder siblings exhibit some vitality, but Ralph Purcell is an almost exact reprise of Roger Foote (*If Death Ever Slept*).

58. "Death of a Demon"
in *Homicide Trinity* (1962)

Victim: Barry Hazen—public relations consultant and blackmailer; shot.

Client: Lucy Hazen—wife of Barry.

Other Principals: Mrs. Victor Oliver—widow of a millionaire broker. Anne Talbot—wife of banker Henry Lewis Talbot. Jules Khoury—inventor. Ambrose Perdis—shipping tycoon. Theodore Weed—assistant to Barry Hazen.

Synopsis: Lucy Hazen offers Wolfe a hundred dollars for a half hour of his time, during which she shows him a gun and declares, "That's the gun I'm going to shoot my husband with." She then asks to see Wolfe's orchids, and while she is on the roof Archie learns from the radio that her husband's body has been found. The police arrest Mrs. Hazen, and Wolfe undertakes her defense. He concentrates his investigation upon Hazen's activities as a blackmailer. Stationed in the Hazen house, Archie surprises a number of people who arrive to search for incriminating evidence, and he blackmails them into gathering in Wolfe's office. Wolfe then devises a stratagem which causes the revelation of the murderer's identity at a second gathering the same evening.

Comment: A fine opening dwindles into a routine case as Wolfe once again resorts to one of his improbably successful stratagems.

59. "Eeny Meeny Murder Mo"
in *Homicide Trinity* (1962)

Victim: Bertha Aaron—legal secretary; strangled.

Client: none.

Other Principals: Lamont Otis, Frank Edey, Miles Heydecker, Gregory Jett—law partners. Ann Paige—associate in the firm of Otis, Edey, etc. Rita Sorell—a golddigger, suing an Otis, Edey, etc. client for divorce.

Synopsis: Bertha Aaron has observed a member of her firm meeting surreptitiously with Rita Sorell. She wants Wolfe to investigate. Wolfe tells Archie to decline the assignment, but when Archie returns to the office, he finds that Miss Aaron has been strangled with one of Wolfe's ties. In order to repair self-esteem, Wolfe undertakes to identify the killer. Wolfe interviews all the partners of the law firm, and Archie visits Rita Sorell. Finally, Wolfe develops a stratagem in which he gathers the principals in his front room while he discovers the murderer by questioning Rita Sorell in his office.

Comment: A standard novella, with an unusual (and unnecessary) use of the front room.

60. "Counterfeit for Murder"
in *Homicide Trinity* (1962)

Victim: Tamiris Baxter—aspiring actress; stabbed.

Client: Hattie Annis—spinster landlady.

Other Principals: Raymond Dell, Noel Ferris, Paul Hannah, Martha Kirk—actors boarding with Hattie Annis.

Synopsis: Hattie Annis, with a strong antipathy to the police, wants Wolfe to investigate ten thousand dollars in counterfeit bills which she has found in the parlor of her boarding house. Archie accompanies her to her building and discovers the body of Tamiris Baxter in the parlor. Hattie refuses to cooperate with the police, and employs Wolfe to make the police "eat dirt." Wolfe questions the principals about their activities and assigns Saul, Fred, and Orrie to pursue various inquiries. He then gathers the principals and the authorities (which include an agent of the Secret Service) and identifies the counterfeiter/murderer.

Comment: Ragged, rich, and salty, Hattie Annis is one of the more colorful characters encountered by Wolfe; her obstinacy is the match of his. See also the altered version, "Assault on a Brownstone," reprinted in *Death Times Three* (see #74).

61. *Gambit* (1962)

Victim: Paul Jerin—master chess player; poisoned.

Client: Sally Blount—daughter of Matthew Blount.

Other Principals: Matthew Blount—President of the Blount Textile Corp. Anna Blount—Bewitching wife of Matthew. Ernst Hausman—retired Wall Street executive. Morton Farrow—Blount Textile vice-president. Charles Yerkes—bank vice-president. Daniel Kalmus—corporation lawyer. Dr. Victor Avery—Blount family physician.

Synopsis: Paul Jerin is poisoned while playing twelve simultaneous chess matches at the Gambit Club. Blount and the four messengers who carried the plays—Hausman, Farrow, Yerkes, and Kalmus—are the main suspects. The police arrest Blount and charge him with the crime. Against the wishes of her father and his lawyer (Kalmus), Sally Blount engages Wolfe to investigate the crime on her father's behalf. Wolfe concludes that Jerin was not the primary target of the attack, and he focuses his attention upon Kalmus. Another murder is committed, and Blount makes a damaging but revealing confession to Archie. Wolfe and Archie both realize the identity of the murderer, but in the absence of evidence, they employ a stratagem which causes the killer to commit suicide.

Comment: The title of the book refers to the scene of the crime (the Gambit Club), the occasion of the crime (the chess match), and the motive for the crime. Although Wolfe's own concluding gambit is rather transparent, the actions and the characters are interesting and the plot is coherent.

The novel opens with a fine scene in which Wolfe systematically annihilates his copy of *Webster's New International Dictionary, Third Edition, Unabridged,* "because it threatens the integrity of the English language."

62. *The Mother Hunt* (1963) 5

Victim: Ellen Tenzer—a spinster who boards babies; strangled.

Client: Lucy Valdon—wealthy widow of Richard Valdon, best-selling author.

Other Principals: Manuel Upton—editor of *Distaff* magazine. Julian Haft—President of Parthenon Press. Leo Bingham—television producer. Willis Krug—literary agent. Carol Mardus—*Distaff* fiction editor, and ex-wife of Willis Krug.

Synopsis: Lucy Valdon employs Wolfe to investigate the maternity of a baby which has been left at her doorstep with a note attributing its paternity to her late husband. Archie traces the infant to Ellen Tenzer, who is murdered shortly after he first encounters her. After questioning Valdon's four principal associates, Wolfe directs an exhaustive and fruitless search for the mother. He then devises a stratagem which does cause the mother to reveal herself, but she too is murdered before she can impart crucial information. Wolfe flees his house in order to escape Inspector Cramer's attempt to arrest him for concealing evidence. He finally gathers the principals in the home of his client and in the presence of Cramer exposes the culprit.

Comment: Archie seems to have an unusually close rapport with Lucy Valdon; the novel is otherwise a typical performance. Unlike many mystery writers (from Sophocles to Ross Macdonald), Stout tends not to exploit genetic identity as a source of dramatic surprises or of thematic preoccupations.

63. "Kill Now—Pay Later"
in *Trio for Blunt Instruments* (1964)

Victims: Dennis Ashby—Vice-President of Mercer's Bobbins, Inc.; defenestrated. Pete Vassos—Greek bootblack; fall from a cliff.

Client: Elma Vassos—stenographer; daughter of Pete.

Other Principals: John Mercer—President of Mercer's Bobbins. Andrew Busch—secretary of the corporation. Philip Horan—salesman. Frances Cox—receptionist. Joan Ashby—widow of Dennis.

Synopsis: Pete Vassos polishes shoes at Wolfe's residence and at the offices of Mercer's Bobbins. He arrives early at Wolfe's and mentions Ashby's sudden demise. He hints that he may have seen something. The following day Vassos's body is found at the bottom of a cliff, and the police surmise that he committed suicide in remorse for killing Ashby (who has been rumored to have seduced Elma Vassos). Elma employs Wolfe to restore her father's reputation (and her own). Wolfe gathers the principals in his office; there his clever deduction of the identity of the murderer is confirmed when Saul Panzer reports that Vassos had written the name of his killer in blood at the base of the cliff.

Comment: The true motive for the crime is announced only as the culprit is identified. Nonetheless, Wolfe's deduction is clever. Saul Panzer's confirmation of the deduction, however, is one of the most baffling episodes in the series. It is unnecessary (Saul has produced other supporting evidence); it is melodramatic in the worst sense; and it is extremely improbable (requiring incredibly poor eyesight on the part of the police who originally retrieved Vassos's body).

64. "Murder Is Corny" 5
in *Trio for Blunt Instruments* (1964)

Victim: Kenneth Faber—cartoonist and temporary farm worker; beaten.

Client: Archie.

Other Principals: Duncan McLeod—upstate farmer who provides Wolfe with fresh corn. Sue McLeod—Duncan's daughter; fashion model. Max Maslow—fashion photographer. Carl Heydt—couturier. Peter Jay—advertising executive.

Synopsis: Inspector Cramer delivers Wolfe's special order of handpicked corn and reports that the regular delivery boy, Kenneth Faber, has been found murdered behind Rusterman's Restaurant. Faber, infatuated with Sue McLeod, had been spreading a rumor that he had gotten her pregnant. Sue McLeod testifies that Archie had been near the scene of the crime. Cramer arrests Archie, then, at Wolfe's instigation, he arrests Sue.

When Archie is released, Wolfe pursues further inquiries. A second box of corn arrives at the brownstone, and Wolfe correctly concludes that it contains dynamite. Wolfe permits the murderer to commit suicide, then explains the case to Inspector Cramer.

Comment: Sexual politics plays an increasing role in the late tales. Here Sue McLeod's declaration of her own virginity is taken—by Archie at least—as an indication of her innocence of the crime of murder (this despite her prevarications which have implicated Archie himself).

"Murder Is Corny" is the third of the Wolfe novellas not to appear in a periodical prior to being published in a book collection (the others being "Poison à la Carte" and "The Rodeo Murder"). Stout ceased to produce for a vanishing market: *Trio for Blunt Instruments* collects the last of the original shorter Wolfe tales.

65. "Blood Will Tell"
in *Trio for Blunt Instruments* (1964)

Victim: Bonny Kirk—estranged wife of Martin Kirk; beaten.

Client: Martin Kirk—architect.

Other Principals: James Neville Vance—wealthy dilettante and enamored of Bonny Kirk. Paul Fougere—vice president of Audivideo and enamored of Bonny Kirk. Rita Fougere—wife of Paul (not enamored of Bonny Kirk).

Synopsis: Archie receives in the mail a blood-stained tie belonging to James Neville Vance. He visits Vance in Greenwich Village to return it, but Vance cannot explain the incident. While Archie is there, the body of Bonny Kirk is discovered in her apartment in the same building. Kirk, a suspect, employs Wolfe to investigate the crime. Wolfe makes inquiries; the police arrest Kirk. Wolfe obtains evidence from the killer's apartment, and, after gathering the principals in his office, turns the culprit over to Inspector Cramer.

Comment: The emotional interrelationships make for an unusually coherent story. The evidence obtained by Wolfe—a bloody lock of hair stored in a glove—recalls the abnormal psychology of *The League of Frightened Men*.

66. *A Right to Die* (1964)

Victim: Susan Brooke—civil rights activist; beaten.

Client: Dunbar Whipple—civil rights activist.

Other Principals: Paul Whipple—assistant professor of anthropology and
father of Dunbar. Kenneth and Dolly Brooke—brother and sister in-
law of Susan. Peter Vaughan—admirer of Susan. Thomas Henchy—
head of the Rights of Citizens Committee (ROCC). Harold Oster—
ROCC attorney. Maud Jordan, Adam Ewing, Cass Faison, Rae Kallman,
Beth Tiger—ROCC staff members.

Synopsis: Paul Whipple, the black serving boy in *Too Many Cooks*, was so
impressed by Wolfe's lecture on citizenship in 1938 that he now turns to
Wolfe in hopes of having him intervene in the proposed marriage of
his twenty-one-year-old son and a white girl, Susan Brooke. From a sense
of debt, Wolfe agrees to look into the matter. Archie begins to investigate Susan's past, but she is suddenly murdered and the police charge
her fiancé with the crime. Wolfe commits himself to Dunbar's defense.
He questions the arrogant Kenneth and Dolly Brooke, and he twice
gathers the ROCC staff in his office. A second murder is committed,
and Wolfe, after reviewing the entire case, realizes the identity of the
murderer. He has the culprit brought to his office and elicits a complete
confession.

Comment: A remarkable performance on two counts: first, the return (and
the progress) of Paul Whipple; and second, the willingness to confront
the issue of race. Although *Too Many Cooks* represented a relatively ad-
vanced treatment of race relations in 1938, the standards had risen considerably by the sixties. Wolfe and Whipple now approach one another
with a mature and mutual respect. In 1938 Archie had been free with
racial slurs; now he resorts to "quote nigger unquote" when transcrib-
ing the speech of the Brookes. Archie even extends his notorious sus-
ceptibility to feminine charms to the black Beth Tiger. *A Right to Die* is
not controversial or polemical, merely tolerant. Paul Whipple has ac-
complished his American Dream, but he—and his son—still face the
American divisions.

The plot seems a bit cottonmouthed, but the disclosure of the
murderer's motives produces some unexpected insights.

67. *The Doorbell Rang* (1965)

Victim: Morris Althaus—freelance writer and investigative journalist; shot.

Client: Rachel Bruner—wealthy widow; head of Bruner Realty.

Other Principals: Sarah Dacos—secretary to Mrs. Bruner. Ivana Althaus—mother of Morris. Marian Hinckley—fiancée of Morris Althaus. Frank Odell—realtor investigated by Morris Althaus. Richard Wragg—head of the FBI's New York City office.

Synopsis: Mrs. Bruner offers Wolfe one hundred thousand dollars (plus a fee and expenses) to force the FBI to cease its unprovoked surveillance of her and her associates. Inspector Cramer, learning of Wolfe's commission, privately informs him that the Police Department is convinced that the FBI was responsible for the murder of Morris Althaus, but that it lacks sufficient positive evidence to sustain a formal charge. Wolfe pursues the Althaus affair. He gathers the principals in his office, and, confident that his residence has been bugged, proclaims his conviction that the FBI is indeed implicated. Through a stratagem, he manages to blackmail the FBI into ending its harassment of Mrs. Bruner. He also provides the police with the evidence that will convict the murderer of Morris Althaus.

Comment: A remarkable polemic against the FBI of J. Edgar Hoover; in *A Right to Die* and *The Doorbell Rang*, Stout exploits his grand mastery of the mystery genre as a vehicle to effectively communicate his serious social concerns. Wolfe strongly endorses the views of Fred Cook in *The FBI Nobody Knows* (1964). Mrs. Bruner's troubles derive in part from the gesture of having mailed copies of the book to ten thousand prominent Americans. Both Inspector Cramer (the police) and Lon Cohen (the press) are awed by Wolfe's determination to defy the Bureau. Everyone else has responded to the Bureau's invasions of privacy with passive outrage. Wolfe's triumph over the intrusive and arrogant bureaucrats is epitomized in a final scene in which Hoover himself is left on Wolfe's doorstep, vainly ringing the bell to gain admission. (Wolfe's indignation is somewhat undermined by his own highly cultivated arrogance and his own selective indifference to the right of privacy. In the very next novel, he surreptitiously records a conversation between Inspector Cramer and a witness.)

Incidental references to Goldwater, Johnson, and the Beatles serve to set the time. Part of Wolfe's stratagem involves a reassembling of the ill-fated dinner party of "Poison à la Carte" (1960). Wolfe produces a nice retort to Mrs. Bruner's challenge regarding his courage: "Afraid? I can dodge folly without backing into fear."

68. *Death of a Doxy* (1966) 4

Victim: Isabel Kerr—kept woman; beaten.

Client: Orrie Cather—detective; object of Isabel Kerr's infatuation.

Other Principals: Avery Ballou—President, Federal Holding Corporation and Isabel's keeper. Stella Fleming—Isabel's respectable sister. Barry Fleming—high school mathematics teacher and Stella's husband. Amy Jackson—"Julie Jacquette," showgirl and friend of Isabel. Dr. Theodore Gamin—admirer of Isabel.

Synopsis: Isabel Kerr has decided to marry Orrie Cather; Orrie has decided to marry a stewardess, Jill Hardy. Archie sneaks into Isabel's apartment intending to retrieve traces of Orrie's liaison with Isabel, but he encounters her corpse. The police arrest Orrie. Wolfe, Archie, Saul Panzer and Fred Durkin agree that Orrie must be innocent and undertake to investigate the crime on his behalf. Avery Ballou's relationship with Isabel remains unknown to the police, but Wolfe learns of it and questions him. Stella Fleming proves to be neurotically obsessed with maintaining the good name of her sister. Wolfe learns that Ballou has been paying blackmail, and he deduces the identity of the blackmailer (and, therefore, of the murderer). He uses Amy Jackson in a maneuver first to force the exposure of the criminal and then to force the death of the criminal.

Comment: Wolfe's crucial deduction is puerile; the blackmailer has pointlessly adopted two pseudonyms, the second of which consists of a fairly obvious allusion to the blackmailer's actual identity. Wolfe reaches his conclusion midway through the novel. The remainder of the action consists of an unconvincing effort to confirm the deduction and a particularly nasty stratagem which leads to the death of the culprit (thus enabling Wolfe to earn a substantial fee for concealing the complicity of Avery Ballou).

Still, the characters are interesting, and the significance of Orrie's predicament is enhanced by his several decades of service as one of Wolfe's auxiliaries. The repartee upholds Stout's high standards, and Wolfe executes another fine rejoinder; Dr. Gamin: "You're grossly overweight." Wolfe nodded. "Seventy pounds. Perhaps eighty. Death will see to that."

69. *The Father Hunt* (1968)

Victim: Elinor Denovo—vice-president of Raymond Thorne Productions; automobile accident.

Client: Amy Denovo—daughter of Elinor.

Other Principals: Raymond Thorne—television producer. Cyrus M. Jarrett—elderly tycoon. Eugene Jarrett—son of Cyrus. Floyd Vance—public relations advisor. Bertram McCray—banker.

Synopsis: Amy Denovo, temporarily working as an assistant to Lily Rowan, employs Wolfe to discover the identity of her father. Following the death of her mother, she received a box containing $264,000 in cash which, a note declared, had been accumulated at the rate of a thousand dollars a month from her father. An inquiry through banking sources leads Wolfe to Cyrus Jarrett. Wolfe broadens his investigation to include the death of Elinor Denovo, whose demise he believes to have been premeditated. Archie and Saul discover the evidence which leads Wolfe to expose the murderer.

Comment: The rather weak plot at least avoids sentimentality. The cast of characters is, as always, economically autonomous, but it is limited enough to allow them to emerge as individuals.

70. *Death of a Dude* (1969)

Victim: Philip Brodell—son of a St. Louis newspaper magnate; shot.

Client: Harvey Greve—wrangler on Lily Rowan's Montana ranch.

Other Principals: Lily Rowan—Archie's long-time companion and owner of the Bar JR Ranch. Carol and Alma Greve—Harvey's wife and daughter. William T. Farnham, Mel Fox, Bert McGee, Sad Peacock, Woodrow Stepanian—Montana ranchers and wranglers. Dr. and Mrs. Amory, Joseph Colihan, Armand DuBois—dudes. Diane Kadany—actress; Lily's guest. Wade Worthy—writer and Lily's guest. Morley Haight—county sheriff. Thomas R. Jessup—county attorney.

Synopsis: On his previous visit to Timberburg, Montana, Philip Brodell had impregnated Alma Greve. On the third day of his current visit, he is discovered shot. When Harvey Greve, whom Archie had met in New York in "The Rodeo Murder," is arrested, Archie writes to Wolfe declaring his intention to extend his Montana vacation until he has exonerated his old friend. After using his influence to question the state attorney general, Wolfe descends upon Lily's ranch and, authorized by Thomas Jessup, begins an investigation. Another principal is murdered, and Sheriff Haight incarcerates Archie. Wolfe uses Saul Panzer to carry out certain inquiries in the East. Saul discovers the identity and the motive of the killer, and Wolfe arranges the arrest so that Jessup receives the credit.

Comment: Only three Wolfe novels transpire outside the vicinity of New York City: *Too Many Cooks* (West Virginia), *The Black Mountain* (Yugoslavia), and *Death of a Dude* (Montana). Stout himself had been making excursions to Montana since 1923. The scene is the most remarkable feature of the novel and, as in the case of *The Black Mountain*, its novelty barely compensates for weak plotting and characterization. Wolfe best exercises his dominance when the narrative is set in a sophisticated, "civilized" scene: a convention, a business, a household—ideally, of course, his own household. He requires a social scale against which to measure the proportions of his intellect. The Bar JR fails to provide such a scale; further, the identity and the motive of the culprit seem contrived, and the multitude of characters renders them generally indistinct. The antagonistic Sheriff Haight and the idiosyncratic Woodrow Stepanian are most individual. There are incidental references to the Vietnam War, the Berkeley protests, and Solzhenitsyn's *The First Circle*.

71. *Please Pass the Guilt* (1973)

Victim: Peter J. Odell—television network (CAN) vice president; bomb.

Client: Madeline Odell—wealthy heiress; wife of Peter.

Other Principals: Cass R. Abbott—President, CAN. Theodore Falk—member, CAN Board of Directors. Amory Browning—vice-president, CAN. Helen Lugos—Browning's secretary. Kenneth Meer—Browning's chief assistant. Dennis Copes—CAN junior executive. Sylvia Venner—CAN television personality.

Synopsis: Kenneth Meer consults Wolfe to seek relief from a compulsion to wipe imaginary blood from his hands. Wolfe offers no cure, but learns that a bomb had exploded in the office of Amory Browning, Meer's superior, killing Peter Odell, who had been competing with Browning to replace the retiring Cass Abbott. Archie maneuvers Mrs. Odell into employing Wolfe to investigate the bombing. Wolfe gathers the principals in his office for an interrogation, then assigns Archie, Saul, Orrie, and Fred to make various inquiries. Wolfe eventually detects a "strikingly suggestive" comment in the testimony of one of the principals, and he uses the comment to force the self-exposure of the murderer.

Comment: *Please Pass the Guilt* epitomizes the defects of the later novels: there is a proliferation of ill-defined, inadequately motivated characters, a general disregard for concrete scene or context (it takes the reader some time to realize that CAN is a television network, not an airline: occupations and professional activities are very abstract), and the plot conceals its weakness through dramatic or ideological digressions (e.g., Meer's improbable Lady Macbeth complex, the incident in which a Jewish infiltrator of an Arab terrorist cell claims the reward offered by Mrs. Odell, or Archie's extended discussion of the etymologies of certain vulgar expressions with the feminist Sylvia Venner). On the other hand, Wolfe and Archie themselves are in good form. There is a nice set of allusions to the Miracle Mets of 1969.

72. *A Family Affair* (1975)

Victims: Pierre Ducos—waiter at Rusterman's Restaurant; bomb. Harvey H. Bassett—President of NATELEC (National Electronics Industries); shot. Lucille Ducos—feminist daughter of Pierre.

Client: none.

Other Principals: Wolfe, Archie, Saul, Orrie, Fred—the "family." Felix Martin—present proprietor of Rusterman's. Philip Corela—sauce chef at Rusterman's. Harvey Bassett's dinner guests at Rusterman's—Albert O. Judd (lawyer), Francis Ackerman (lawyer), Roman Vilar (security expert), Ernest Urquhart (lobbyist), Willard K. Hahn (banker), Benjamin Igoe (electronics engineer).

Synopsis: Pierre Ducos arrives at Wolfe's residence late one night, insisting that his life has been threatened and that he must speak to Wolfe directly. Archie declares that he must wait until morning, but allows him to spend the night in the spare bedroom. Moments later, a miniature bomb explodes in Pierre's room. (Bombs seem to be the preferred weapon of the seventies.) Wolfe vows to exact vengeance and begins an investigation. Philip Corela connects Pierre's death with a slip of paper left behind at a dinner meeting held by Harvey Bassett at Rusterman's. Wolfe pursues inquiries at the home of Pierre's father and daughter, and he gathers the dinner guests in his office for questioning. Lucille Ducos is murdered. Wolfe, Archie, Saul, Orrie, and Fred are arrested and are imprisoned over a weekend. The police suspend Wolfe's license. The members of Wolfe's "family" come to realize the identity of the murderer. They conspire to force the killer to commit suicide with a second bomb.

Comment: Despite a weak plot—the crucial slip of paper lacks credibility and the actions and motives of Pierre and his daughter seem arbitrary—the Wolfe saga ends on a strong note. In *Fer-de-Lance,* Wolfe, with a cavalier disregard for human life, adopted a "suicide solution" as a romantic gesture: he exercised Providential authority in arranging the "happy" deaths of two of the principals. The suicide solution of *A Family Affair* is neither romantic nor happy. Wolfe does not usurp authority; rather, the "family" resolutely decides that suicide is the only acceptable outcome to the moral situation which they face.

The Watergate Affair provides a powerful and pervasive context for the drama. Wolfe declares: "I would have given all of my orchids—well, most of them—to have an effective hand in the disclosure of the malfeasance of Richard Nixon." Archie, Lily Rowan, Orrie Cather, and Harvey Bassett at various times express or imply their contempt for the former president. Indeed, the occasion of Bassett's dinner party was his effort to plot further retribution against Nixon. (Stout himself clearly shared these sentiments.) And there is an explicit contrast between the corruption of Nixon's "Palace Guard" (Wolfe is reading Dan Rather's book of that title) and the integrity of Wolfe's "family." Archie draws the comparison: "Five men being tried now in Washington for conspiracy to obstruct justice—Haldeman, Ehrlichman, Mitchell, Mardian, and Parkinson. Five being charged here with conspiracy to obstruct justice—Wolfe, Goodwin, Panzer, Durkin, and Cather." The five in New York dedicate themselves—successfully—to vindicating their honor.

The emphasis upon the resilient virtue of the world over which Wolfe presides offers a fitting conclusion to the series. As he departs for the last time, an irate Inspector Cramer declares: "I'm going home and try to get some sleep. You probably have never had to try to get some sleep. You never will." But the extra-judicial justice which Wolfe imposes in *A Family Affair* does have a price—a special, personal price. There is an earned poignance to Wolfe's last words: "Will you bring brandy, Archie? And two glasses. If Fritz is up, bring him and three glasses. We'll try to get some sleep."

73. "Frame-Up for Murder"
in *Death Times Three* (1985)

Victims, etc.: the same as in "Murder Is No Joke" (see #50).

Comment: In 1985 well-known Stout critic and biographer John McAleer edited a posthumous collection, *Death Times Three*, containing three "largely new" Nero Wolfe novellas, with a very useful introduction by McAleer. The first story, "Bitter End," hitherto available only in its inaccessible original periodical appearance, has already been covered here in its proper chronological order (see *#9*). The other two stories, including "Frame-Up," are more or less altered versions of tales already collected in previous novella volumes.

"Frame-Up for Murder" is an expansion of "Murder Is No Joke," undertaken at the request of *The Saturday Evening Post*, which published the novella under the new title in June-July 1958. The original, shorter version had already been published under its first title in *And Four To Go*, a Wolfe collection, in February 1958.

The only significant difference between the two tales lies in the character of Fiona Gallant. In reducing her age and enlarging her role, Stout did improve the story. In the new version she is young and attractive, with several pages being devoted to her efforts to enlist Archie's cooperation in obtaining Wolfe's assistance. All of the action necessary to the plot remains identical in both versions. McAleer notes that at one time Stout intended Carl Drew to be the villain.

74. "Assault on a Brownstone"
in *Death Times Three* (1985)

Victim: Hattie Annis—spinster landlady; hit-and-run accident.

Client: None.

Other Principals: Tamaris Baxter, Raymond Dell, Noel Ferris, Paul Hannah, Martha Kirk—actors boarding with Hattie Annis.

Synopsis: Hattie Annis is killed shortly after leaving a package with Archie. When the package proves to contain counterfeit money, and when the Secret Service agent pursuing that money commits insufferable intrusions into Wolfe's household, Wolfe undertakes to expose the murderer. He devises a stratagem which leads Archie to the discovery of the villain in Hattie Annis's boarding house.

Comment: The first pages of "Assault" are identical with those of "Counterfeit for Murder" (see #60), and the setting and characters remain the same. As John J. McAleer explains, having completed "Assault" (the title is evidently McAleer's), Stout decided to rewrite, changing the victim from Hattie Annis to Tamaris, and thus radically altering the plot. Although Tamaris is an appealing figure, the elaboration of Hattie Annis's colorful character justifies Stout's preference for the second version. "Assault" does offer two minor pleasures: Archie briefly plays the part of the dismissed detective; and the Secret Service's rude search of the brownstone anticipates the greater intrusion performed by the FBI in *The Doorbell Rang*.

II.

BONNER, FOX, CRAMER, HICKS, and OTHERS

INTRODUCTION

Although Nero Wolfe rapidly established himself as one of the preeminent fictional detectives, Rex Stout made several gestures toward inaugurating another series protagonist during his first decade as a writer of popular fiction. In part, his motive was commercial. The first of his non-Wolfe detective novels, *The Hand in the Glove* (1937), was composed in response to his publisher's concern that the market might not be able to absorb more than one Nero Wolfe novel per year. But there was doubtless also an artistic consideration. Prior to the publication of *Fer-de-Lance* in 1934, Stout had published four "serious" novels which had earned him comparisons with D. H. Lawrence, William Faulkner, and Aldous Huxley. Two of the novels he published after 1934—*O Careless Love!* (1935) and *Mr. Cinderella* (1938)—also fall into this more respectable category. If in his later years Stout was generally content to produce routine variations upon the long-standing Wolfe formulas, in his first years he actively experimented with more radical alternatives to those formulas, both without the genre and within it. His new detectives could not be less like Nero Wolfe: one is a woman, one a policeman; all are extremely mobile; the adventures of all are narrated in the third person. And, very much unlike Nero Wolfe, they all proved to be very short-lived.

The chief attractions of the Wolfe novels are the commanding presence of Wolfe and the provocative voice of Archie. To compensate for the loss of these features, the non-Wolfe novels place a greater emphasis upon developing more fully the cast of incidental characters and upon maintaining a faster pace of action. In both respects, the non-Wolfe novels are superior to the Wolfe adventures. Stout himself once described *Double for Death* as his "best, technically, detective story." But technical perfection was evidently not a priority for Stout's readers, and after 1941 Stout devoted himself exclusively to the adventures of Nero Wolfe.

Theodolinda (Dol) Bonner, the first of the un-Wolfean detectives, is almost an anti-Wolfe. She is a woman; she is young; she is slim and attractive. Wolfe frequently expresses his antipathy toward women; Dol Bonner, following a romantic disappointment, has resolved to mistrust all men. Wolfe is a wealthy eccentric; Dol is a commonplace working girl. Like Wolfe, she is a professional private detective, but unlike him, she is—excepting her femininity—a typical private detective: she operates an agency, she worries about collecting fees and paying rent, she makes house calls. She even employs a sort of anti-Archie Goodwin in the person of her partner, Sylvia Raffray. Sylvia does not narrate *The Hand in the Glove* (1937), and unlike Archie, she is independently wealthy. But she is a trustworthy accomplice and, like Archie, she is susceptible to the attractions of the opposite sex.

Although it would be impossible to mistake Dol Bonner for Nero Wolfe, they both do inhabit the same world. Indeed, all of Stout's detectives occupy a common territory: New York City and Westchester County. Not surprisingly, the non-Wolfe protagonists are more inclined to undertake excursions into the county, but the terrain is basically a familiar one. Wolfe and his competitors patronize the same restaurants and antagonize the same authorities. Dol, for example, rather improbably encounters Inspector Cramer at the end of her case. (And she herself will later reappear in several of Wolfe's cases.) In addition to sharing common places and common persons, Stout's detectives also share a common social milieu. The clients, victims, and suspects in *The Hand in the Glove* comprise Stout's standard assortment of wealthy capitalists, young lovers, wives, artists, academics, and reporters. Wolfe himself might easily have accepted the commission to expose the person who strangled the president of the Commercial Chemicals Corporation on the grounds of his lavish Westchester County estate.

For the un-Wolfean protagonist of *Red Threads* (1939), Stout appropriated Inspector Cramer, whom he had already established in the Wolfe novels as the pedestrian antithesis to the great detective. Stout was not inclined to research the background required to produce a realistic police procedural, nor could he be bothered to provide Cramer with a private history or a domestic environment or even a first name (though he does, in passing, give him a teenage daughter), nor was he about to develop Cramer into a striking personality, thus ruining him as a phlegmatic foil to Wolfe. And so, ironically, Cramer plays a much less impressive role as the star of his own novel than he does as a supporting character in the Wolfe series. Cramer functions adequately as an antagonist; as a protagonist he is quite colorless. That the circumstances of the murder which he is called upon to investigate are among the most *outré* in any of Stout's novels only serves to accentuate his own insufficiency.

In *Mountain Cat* (1939) Stout sought to escape the shadow of Nero Wolfe by setting the mystery in distant Wyoming (thirty years later he would actually place Wolfe in the same vicinity in *Death of a Dude*.) At the same time he also chose to escape from the genre of the detective story itself. *Mountain Cat* is a murder mystery, but no detective—amateur or professional—organizes the investigation of the crime. Instead, various characters make their partial contributions to the elucidation of the mystery, until at the dramatic conclusion one of them finally puts the pieces together and solves the puzzle.

In *Double for Death* (1939), Stout seemed at last to have discovered a second viable premise for a detective series. The hero, Tecumseh Fox, interested his creator and his audience sufficiently to justify two encores. Fox represents a return to the notion of the eccentric, masculine, private detective, but his genus is vulpine rather than lupine. Where Wolfe is fat and immobile, Fox is slight, gregarious, and active. Instead of a tightly regulated Manhattan brownstone, Fox maintains his peculiar menagerie, The Zoo, in the country. But like Dol Bonner and Inspector Cramer, he lives in Wolfe's world. He too dines at Rusterman's, and the Westchester County authorities whom he encounters are the same as those confronted by Wolfe on his occasional forays north. And Fox does earn the very odd distinction of having been translated into Nero Wolfe when Stout revised Fox's second adventure, *Bad for Business* (1940), into the Wolfe novella, "Bitter End" (1940).

Fox's debut was auspicious. *Double for Death*, with its abundance of duplicities, is a cleverly plotted tale. *Bad for Business* is a solid mystery, but a comparison of the Fox and Wolfe versions emphasizes the advantage of Wolfe's more impressive personality. The most memorable scene of "Bitter End" is the one Stout added to the beginning in which Wolfe happens to sample some of the tainted *paté* and spits a mouthful all over his kitchen and Archie. The defect of Fox's indefinite character is fully apparent in his third case, *The Broken Vase* (1941), and his consequent retirement was mourned neither by creator nor audience.

Stout made one other attempt to establish a second-string detective, but Alphabet Hicks is, if anything, a pale echo of the pallid Tecumseh Fox. *The Sound of Murder* (1941) is a solid mystery, but the uninspiring hero and the disembodied narration again fail to match in interest the vital combination of Nero Wolfe and Archie Goodwin.

The President Vanishes (1934) occupies an equivocal position in Stout's canon. It seems to straddle the rather arbitrary categories of the serious and the popular novel. Its primary purpose is undoubtedly serious: to warn the nation against the perils of a populist fascism and of what Stout precociously saw as a military-industrial complex. The novel actually anticipates by a year Sinclair Lewis's dramatization of the same prospect in *It Can't Happen Here*. And the panoramic structure of *The President Vanishes*—with its selective glimpses into the lives of the wealthy, the powerful, the fanatical, the responsible, and the just plain folk—is far more ambitious than that of Stout's normal mysteries. But the action is distinctly melodramatic. There is a crime and an investigation; there are clues and misdirections; there is a surprise ending. And so, with reservations, *The President Vanishes* has been included among the non-Wolfe mysteries.

"A substitute shines brightly as a king / Until a king be by." The contrast between Stout's Wolfean and non-Wolfean mysteries illustrates Portia's observation. The non-Wolfean novels are, at their worst, competent detective stories. But Nero Wolfe is the true king, the ratiocinative Sun King around whom a credible fictional realm might revolve. Dol Bonner, Inspector Cramer, Tecumseh Fox, and Alphabet Hicks find themselves in some unusual and interesting situations and in the company of some unusual and interesting persons, but their world never seems quite as vivid as the one Nero Wolfe ruled over for forty years.

SYNOPSES

75. *The President Vanishes* (1934)

Victim: President Stanley.

Principal Detectives: Lewis Warden—Secretary of the Interior. Philip Skinner—Chief of the Secret Service. Chick Moffat—Secret Service Agent.

Other Principals: Lillian Stanley—wife of the president. Alma Cronin—assistant secretary to Mrs. Stanley. Harry Brownell—secretary to the president. Robert A. Molleson vice president. Lincoln Lee—American fascist; leader of the Gray Shirts. Val Orcutt—delivery boy.

Senators: Corcoran, Allen, Tilney, Reid, Sterling.

Cabinet members: Oliver (War), Snick (Commerce), Liggett (State), Billings (Agriculture), Davis (Attorney General).

Tycoons: George Milton, Daniel Cullen, Martin Drew, D. L. Voorman, Hartley Grinnell.

Synopsis: For more than a year, a world war has been fought in Europe and the Far East. American capitalists and the congressmen they control (three hundred and four Representatives and fifty-nine senators) demand that America enter the conflict. Pacificist organizations (principally the Communists) protest this militarism, but are overwhelmed by Lincoln Lee's fascist Gray Shirts who run riot in the streets. Hours before he is to address the hostile Congress on the issue of war and peace, the president vanishes. The cabinet convenes and appoints Lewis Warden to supervise the search for the president. Suspicion focuses first upon the fascists, but no definite evidence can be discovered. As the nation's war hysteria begins to dissipate in its concern for the president, the tycoons begin to conspire with sympathetic senators and certain military leaders to force the installation of a new pro-war administration under Vice President Molleson. At the last moment, Chick Moffat dramatically rescues the president and shoots a villain. The president then takes advantage of "this modern invention, radio" to discuss the pressing problem of war and peace. The nation gratefully accepts his restored leadership.

Comment: *The President Vanishes* is more of a polemic than a mystery. The actual purpose of the kidnaping plot and certain details of its execution are extremely improbable. The large cast of characters—comprising a panoramic anatomy of American society—and the cinematic cuts from episode to episode enhance the suspense of the story, but diminish its coherence. If there is a protagonist, it is Washington, D.C.

There is an impressive villain; Lincoln Lee is one of Stout's most realistic portrayals of human malignancy. Lee is a genuine fanatic, and Stout pays him and his Gray Shirts the compliment of respecting the sincerity of their misguided views. Far less sincere is the second set of villains, the tycoons and their congressional lackeys. Because they are so numerous, they are less fully realized as concrete evils, but the significance of their actions is unmistakable. Stout hammers his point home: "Ordinarily a hundred men rule the United States . . . . Many of them regretted the necessity [of war]; but when their loans to belligerents were endangered, their shiploads of munitions stopped or destroyed, their foreign investments wiped out, their profits annihilated and their market holdings reduced to pitiful fractions war was inevitable. Too bad, but inevitable. They had forthwith communicated with the persons who exist for that purpose; editors, legislators, radio executives, clergymen, professors, patriots." This indictment constitutes the main theme of the novel. *The President Vanishes* is a melodramatic warning against the forces which Stout saw as threatening the stability of American democracy.

76. *The Hand in the Glove* (1937)

Detective: Theodolinda (Dol) Bonner.

Victim: Peter Lewis Storrs—President of the Commercial Chemicals Corporation.

Client: Peter Lewis Storrs.

Other Principals: Cleo Audrey Storrs—mystically inclined wife of P. L. Storrs. Janet Storrs—poetically inclined daughter of P. L. Storrs. Sylvia Raffray—heiress and partner of Dol Bonner. Martin Foltz—Sylvia's fiancé. Leonard Chisholm—newspaper reporter. Steven Zimmerman—assistant professor of psychology. George Leo Ranth—prophet of the League of the Occidental Sakti. Wolfram de Roode—Martin Foltz's estate keeper.

Authorities: Daniel O. Sherwood, county prosecutor. Colonel Brissenden, state police. Inspector Cramer, New York City homicide.

Synopsis: Sylvia Raffray will receive a three million dollar inheritance when she turns twenty-one in three months, but meanwhile P. L. Storrs, her beloved guardian, insists that she repudiate her recently formed partnership with Dol Bonner. Storrs himself then employs Dol to investigate the background of the charlatan, George Leo Ranth, with the purpose of convincing his eccentric wife to abandon her guru. At the same time, Martin Foltz commissions her agency to determine who has been strangling pheasants and rabbits on his country estate (which happens to border that of P. L. Storrs). All of the principals gather at Buchhaven, Storrs' estate, but their pleasant afternoon is disrupted when Dol finds the body of their host dangling from a wire noose. The police arrive and conclude that the body must have been pulled into position by a person wearing gloves. There are no alibis, but there is a surfeit of motives, threats, and falsehoods. Dol Bonner cleverly discovers where the incriminating gloves have been hidden, and she deduces who has hidden them. She also deduces the identity of the killer, but is too late to prevent a second murder. Finally she arranges a private conversation with the villain, analyzes the psychology of the case, and is rescued from an attack by the police. The killer confesses to the authorities.

Comment: The plotting is adequate, but the novel is most noteworthy for its characters. Mrs. Storrs is a marvelous misty mystic; the killer is a striking psychotic. Each of the characters seems to make an unexpected gesture or response which enables him or her to escape the stereotype to which he or she otherwise obviously belongs. They are generic characters in the best sense, familiar but individual.

Though Dol Bonner does not dominate the action, she is an attractive figure: twenty-five; handsome, with caramel-colored eyes; self-reliant; the daughter of a bankrupted Wall Street financier who has committed suicide; betrayed by her fiancé; sole support of her younger brother; a good friend. She has two major connections with the world of Nero Wolfe: Inspector Cramer appears belatedly (and gratuitously) in *The Hand in the Glove*, and Dol plays a minor role in several of Wolfe's cases in the late 1950s ("Too Many Detectives," *Plot It Yourself*).

77. *Mountain Cat* (1939)

Victims: Charlie Brand—grubstaker; shot. Mrs. Brand—Charlie's wife; apparent suicide; poisoned. Daniel Jackson—grubstaker; shot. Rev. Dr. Rufus Toale—pious minister; shot.

Other Principals: Delia Brand—daughter and Rhythmic Movement instructor. Clara Brand—daughter and employed in a grubstaking office. Quinby Pellett—taxidermist and uncle of Delia and Clara. Wynne Cowles—"millionaire playgirl"; the Mountain Cat. Lemuel Sammis—politically powerful old boy and grubstaker. Evelina Sammis—wife of Lemuel. Amy Jackson—wife of Daniel Jackson and daughter of the Sammises. Tyler Dillon—young lawyer. Squint Hurley—prospector.

Authorities: Frank Phelan—Chief of Police, Cody, Wyoming. Bill Tuttle—Park County Sheriff. Ed Baker—Park County Attorney. Kenneth Chambers—Silverside County Attorney.

Synopsis: Two years after the unsolved murder of her father and shortly after the apparent suicide of her mother, Delia Brand purchases ammunition for his pistol and announces her intention to kill a man. Before she can act, she learns that Dan Jackson has fired her sister Clara from her job at his grubstaking office. When Delia visits Jackson's office to protest this injustice, she discovers that he has been killed by a shot fired from her revolver. She is arrested, but several men set to work on her behalf: her uncle, Quinby Pellett; her father's old partner, Lem Sammis; and the man who loves her, Ty Dillon. They eventually succeed in proving that her gun had been stolen from her prior to the murder and that the fatal bullet was of a different brand from that which Delia had purchased.

Delia is convinced that Rufus Toale's ostensibly consolatory ministrations actually precipitated her mother's suicide. Shortly after her release from arrest, Toale, badly wounded, calls upon her and dies in her parlor. Suspicion again focuses upon Delia and Clara. Political forces, including Sammis, the state governor, and a U.S. senator, attempt to influence the murder investigation. Toale's dying words and information obtained from the prospector once tried for the murder of her father lead Delia to realize the identity of the killer. She consults with Wynne Cowles. Finally she enters the killer's house, discovers incriminating evidence, confronts the killer, and is relieved by the arrival of the authorities.

Comment: No single character dominates the action of the novel, but two women seem to be the central figures. Wynne Cowles is a strong but elusive personality: independent (currently arranging her latest divorce), fascinating, imperial, beautiful, disarming. Delia Brand has the largest role. Her ambiguous feelings of revenge and loyalty, love and betrayal are the most fully developed. Some of the minor characters are also solidly imagined, but there seems to be a certain redundancy. There are two sheriffs and two prosecutors. When Delia is arrested, she finds two competing lawyers working on her behalf. There are two sisters; both parents are dead; two boys are involved in the mystery surrounding the ammunition purchased by Delia.

The scene of the action is Cody, Wyoming. Stout had set his 1933, non-detective novel, *Forest Fire*, in the same area, and in the *Death of a Dude* (1969) he would send Nero Wolfe to nearby Montana. There is, however, little vivid evocation of the western landscape in *Mountain Cat*, and Stout is typically vague about the details of the business of grub-staking. Circumstantial realism is never a primary value in his story-telling.

78. *Double for Death* (1939)

Detective: Tecumseh Fox.

Victims: Ridley Thorpe—head of Thorpe Control; shot. Corey Arnold—Thorpe's look-alike stand-in; shot.

Client: Andrew Grant—delitescent writer; advertising copywriter.

Other Principals: Nancy Grant—daughter of Andrew and fashion model. Jeffrey Thorpe—son of Ridley. Miranda Pemberton—divorced daughter of Ridley Thorpe. Dorothy Duke—mistress of Ridley Thorpe. Henry Jordan—father of Dorothy Duke. Luke Wheer—Ridley Thorpe's black valet. Vaughn Kester—Ridley Thorpe's confidential secretary. Dan Pavey—Tecumseh Fox's "vice president" and general factotum.

Authorities: District Attorney Derwin; Colonel Brissenden.

Synopsis: Nancy Grant visits Fox on his Westchester County estate to ask that he assist her father, who has been accused of murdering Ridley Thorpe at his country cottage. Fox investigates, deduces that the victim was not really Ridley Thorpe, and employs a stratagem which enables him to locate the true Thorpe. Thorpe, who has been trysting with Dorothy Duke, offers Fox fifty thousand dollars to arrange a satisfactory excuse for his failure to communicate with the authorities. Fox rises to the occasion with a very complicated, but completely successful maneuver.

Thorpe invites Fox to his country estate and employs the detective to investigate the murder of his stand-in. Most of the other principals also happen to be visiting the estate the same day, thus all become prime suspects when the true Thorpe is truly killed. A variety of clues and motives implicate everyone (including Fox himself when it is discovered that the murder weapon is his property). Fox eventually focuses upon the crucial indications and obtains a confession from the murderer.

Comment: "TWO Ridley Thorpes! TWO beautiful suspects! TWO hot-headed suitors! TWO murder weapons! TWO corpses!"—as this blurb from the paperback edition suggests, the title *Double for Death* is well-chosen. Despite some fortuitous movements on the parts of the murder weapons, the plotting is ingenious, and the characters comprise a distinctive lot. Nancy Grant is another lovely-and-self-reliant-heroine, but the "TWO hot-headed suitors," one of whom is Fox's factotum (the other, Jeffrey Thorpe, a typical impetuous rich boy), lend color to her romance.

This, the first of his three cases, is the only one in which Fox's personality really dominates the action. His manipulation of Thorpe's alibi, his fronting of the authorities, his patter (especially with Dan Pevey), and his nervous energy contribute to this effect. A few brief scenes of Fox at home provide the fullest portrait of his eccentric farm establishment, The Zoo. Judging by *Double for Death*, Tecumseh Fox might well have become a rural, bohemian Wolfe.

79. *Red Threads* (1939)

Detective: Inspector Cramer, New York City Homicide.

Victim: Valentine Carew—multimillionaire; beaten.

Other Principals: Guy Straightfoot Carew—Valentine's half-Cherokee son and heir. Jean Farris—textile designer and object of Guy Carew's affections. Eileen Delany—Jean Farris's partner. Portia Tritt—publicity counselor and Valentine Carew's fiancée. Leo Krantz—textile importer. Amory Buysse—curator of the National Indian Museum. Woodrow Wilson—Cherokee Indian companion of Valentine Carew. Mr. and Mrs. Melville Barth—Wall Street magnate and his socialite wife.

Other Authorities: Westchester District Attorney Anderson, New York City District Attorney Skinner, and Police Commissioner Humbert.

Synopsis: Inspector Cramer is recalled from a hunting vacation in Canada to assist in the investigation of the month-old murder of Valentine Carew. Though the crime took place at the Carew estate in Westchester County, the county district attorney has requested the aid of the New York City authorities. Carew was murdered in the shrine which he had built to his Indian wife, Tsianinia, and to which he repaired in a daybreak ritual whenever an important decision was required of him. On the day his corpse was discovered in the shrine, all of the principals had been guests at the estate. The police have one clue: a strand of red thread caught in the dead man's fist. At a dinner party given by the Barths and attended by all of the principals, Jean Farris wears a costume which contains this thread. During the evening, someone knocks her unconscious and steals her jacket and skirt.

Inspector Cramer doggedly interviews each of the principals. When the problem of Jean Farris's costume directs his attention toward her, he arrests her as a material witness and grills her until she collapses. When Guy Carew comes to Jean's defense, Cramer uses a simple device to break down his alibi and then charges Carew with the murder. Jean Farris refuses to accept this indictment and undertakes a provocative investigation of her own. She comes to certain conclusions and takes her evidence to Cramer. Supported by other principals, she pricks him to further inquiry. Ignoring political interference from his superiors, Cramer pursues these new leads and forces a confession from the killer.

Comment: Even when he escapes Wolfe's shadow, Cramer does not shine very brightly. He does administer an impressive third degree, but as always he manages to arrest the wrong person. Prompted by Jean Farris, he at least corrects his own error.

The plot is complex and coherent, but several of the premises are odd. The crime and most of the significant action take place outside of Cramer's jurisdiction. The murder is a month old, and it seems to have had no great emotional impact upon any of the survivors. And the scene of the crime is bizarre: a marble temple housing the remains of Tsianinia. Carew has drilled 365 holes in the wall. If the dawning sun illuminates the face of his wife's body, he will think only of her and refuse to undertake any new project (such as marriage to Portia Tritt). The subjects of textiles and Indians provide some specific background materials for the story. The three Other Authorities are familiar figures from the Wolfe series.

80. *Bad for Business* (1940)

Detective: Tecumseh Fox.

Victim: Arthur Tingley—head of Tingley's Tidbits; slashed throat.

Client: Amy Duncan—Tingley's niece and probationary private detective.

Other Principals: Leonard Cliff—vice president of P & B (Provisions and Beverages). Gwendolyn Yates—in charge of production at Tingley's. Sol Fry—in charge of sales at Tingley's. Carne Murphy—forewoman at Tingley's. Philip Tingley—Arthur's adopted son. Guthrie Judd—multimillionaire owner of Consolidated Foods. Martha Judd—Guthrie's sister. Dol Bonner—head of a detective agency.

Authority: Inspector Damon.

Synopsis: Arthur Tingley has employed Dol Bonner to discover who has been adulterating his titbits with quinine. Suspicion centers upon P & Band Consolidated Foods, both of which have made offers to take over Tingley's. Dol assigns her new operative, Amy Duncan, to make friends with Leonard Cliff of P & B. Amy encounters emotional complications in connection with Cliff, with her uncle Arthur Tingley, and even with Tecumseh Fox, whom she literally runs into on the street. One evening she visits her uncle's downtown factory. She is knocked unconscious and awakes to discover Arthur Tingley's corpse. She instinctively calls upon Fox for help. He comes to the rescue and travels around the city questioning the principals. He uncovers a complex plot involving the natural parents of Philip Tingley. Finally he solves the problem of the quinined titbits and deduces the identity of the killer. Fox arranges for Inspector Damon to gather the principals at the murder scene and there he reveals the criminal.

Comment: Though there is inevitably more circumstantial detail in *Bad for Business*, the plot and characters are substantially the same as those of the Wolfe novella, "Bitter End" (q.v.), which was derived from it. The only major change has been to attach Amy Duncan to Dol Bonner's agency (instead of to P & B), and this serves primarily to make her uneasy romantic relationship with Leonard Cliff more entertaining. The killer in both versions is the same.

The plot and the characters are satisfactory. Philip Tingley emerges most notably as a malcontented political enthusiast who has embraced a sect dedicated to the principle of "womon" ("work-money"). Fox himself receives no further development as a character; his country estate is barely alluded to. He continues to be amusing, but he seems to be ad libbing: his responses are quick-witted, but he fails to communicate a moral authority of the sort embodied in the character of Nero Wolfe.

81. *The Broken Vase* (1941)

Detective: Tecumseh Fox.

Victims: Lawton Mowbray—manager of musicians; apparent suicide; defenestration. Jan Tusar—violinist; apparent suicide; shot. Perry Durham—dilettante son of Mrs. Pomfret by her first marriage; poisoned.

Other Principals: Mrs. Irene Durham Pomfret—wealthy matron and patroness of the arts. Henry Pomfret—collector and second husband of Mrs. Pomfret. Dora Mowbray—Tusar's accompanists and Lawton Mowbray's daughter. Garda Tusar—Jan Tusar's fiery sister. Felix Bech—Jan Tusar's teacher and coach. Theodore Gill—publicity manager. Adolph Koch—dress manufacturer and patron of the arts. Hebe Heath—actress. Diego Zorilla—former pianist and Fox's friend.

Authority: Inspector Damon.

Synopsis: Several months after her father's suicide, Dora Mowbray agrees to accompany Jan Tusar on the piano at his Carnegie Hall debut. Fox, who has contributed toward the purchase of a Stradivarius for Tusar, attends the recital with Diego Zorilla. Tusar's performance is execrable, and during the intermission he shoots himself. The Stradivarius disappears. Mrs. Pomfret insists that everyone who had been involved with Tusar attend a meeting at her midtown mansion. She announces that the violin has been returned anonymously, and she asks Fox to investigate the circumstances. Fox pursues his inquiry, discovers that someone had poured varnish into the instrument (thus ruining the recital and thus precipitating Tusar's suicide), and at a second convening of the principals, declares his intention to expose the criminal. While he is questioning the first of the principals, Perry Dunham is poisoned.

When Inspector Damon fails to make an arrest within the week, Mrs. Pomfret employs Fox to discover the murderer of her son. Fox investigates various aspects of the case, including Hebe Heath's brief, dramatic flight to Mexico, an apparent attempt to abduct Dora Mowbray; a vase stolen from Henry Pomfret's collection; and the secret romantic life of Garda Tusar. At a third convocation of the principals at the Dunham mansion, he exposes the killer.

Comment: Neither the character of the detective nor the revelations of the plot supply a principle of coherence to this third Fox mystery. Fox himself has become a virtually disembodied inquirer, and the motives

77

and the methods which he uncovers are simply incredible. The characters represent a rather mechanical collection of stereotypes, and their interrelationships are unconvincing. The style of the novel reflects Stout's normal fluency, but it is easy to see why booksellers urged him to concentrate upon Nero Wolfe.

82. *The Sound of Murder*
(originally: *Alphabet Hicks*) (1941)

Detective: Alphabet Hicks—a disbarred lawyer.

Victims: Martha Cooper—former actress; beaten. George Cooper—husband of Martha; shot.

Client: Judith Dundee—wife of R. I. Dundee.

Other Principals: R. I. Dundee—head of R. I. Dundee & Company. Ross Dundee—impetuous son of R. I. and Judith Dundee. Heather Gladd—sister of Martha Cooper and secretary to R. I. Dundee. Herman Brager—research scientist for R. I. Dundee & Co. James Vail—head of Republic Products Corp.

Authorities: Manny Beck, Chief of Westchester County Detectives. Ralph Corbett, Westchester County District Attorney.

Synopsis: Judith Dundee employs Hicks to investigate her husband's allegations that she has been passing industrial secrets to his chief competitor, Jimmy Vail. Hicks happens to overhear a woman whose voice is identical to that of Mrs. Dundee, and he follows this stranger to the Dundee home-cum-laboratory in Westchester County. While he speaks to Heather Gladd, the woman (who proves to be Heather's sister, Martha) is murdered. Hicks learns that Dundee's evidence against his wife—a sonotel recording disc of her speaking to Vail—has been lost. Through his sympathy with the lovely Heather, Hicks involves himself in the murder investigation by abetting in the escape of the chief suspect, George Cooper.

Hicks, travelling back and forth between the county and the city, eventually locates the missing sonotel disc. Cooper is killed, and Hicks continues to intrigue with Heather. Some of his plans miscarry. He joins all of the principals (except Brager) in Judith Dundee's city apartment. Jimmy Vail demonstrates the probable guilt of one of the principals; Hicks develops the case against a second. Hicks then insists that all of the principals accompany him back to the laboratory in Westchester County, and there he conclusively identifies the murderer.

Comment: Though the plot depends upon three fundamental and improbable coincidences—the date of Martha Cooper's arrival, the sound of her voice, and Hicks happening to hear her—it is otherwise well-planned. The title suggests both the motive for the crime and the means of its detection.

Hicks is a fairly nondescript protagonist whose single, meager idiosyncrasy consists in affecting acronymic business cards (e.g., "A. Hicks, M.S.O.T.P.B.O.M."=Melancholy Spectator of the Psychic Bellyache of Mankind). Heather Gladd and Ross Dundee form yet another of Stout's lovely-working-girl/callow-rich-boy pairs. Hicks forwards one half of his retainer to the British War Relief and, without evidence, accuses the murderer of subsidizing Nazi propaganda.

83. "By His Own Hand"
in *Eat, Drink, and Be Buried* (1956)

Detective: Alphabet Hicks.

Victim: Adam Nicoll—television and cinema actor; poisoned.

Client: none.

Other Principals: Paul Griffin—author and creator of Kevin Kay. Barry Maddox—Broadway producer. Ernest Levitan—Broadway actor. Amy Quong—actress. Cynthia Nicoll—wife of Adam Nicoll and former wife of Barry Maddox.

Authority: Purley Stebbins.

Synopsis: The novelist Paul Griffin has created the very popular series characters, Kevin Kay and his female sidekick, Cricket. Adam Nicoll and Amy Quong have become identified with the roles in movies and on television. Prompted by Barry Maddox, Griffin writes a play, and Ernest Levitan is engaged to perform the Kevin Kay role on stage. Outraged, Adam Nicoll flies in from Los Angeles. Hicks attends a dinner party at Griffin's apartment, where all of the principals meet, and where Griffin's generous offer to compensate Nicoll seems to solve the difficulty. The next morning, Nicoll is poisoned. Purley Stebbins questions Hicks about the case. Shortly after Stebbins leaves, Paul Griffin telephones Hicks and invites him to meet with the principals at his apartment. Hicks arrives and immediately announces that he knows the identity of the killer. He explains his reasoning and obtains a confession.

Comment: Hicks's deduction is not very convincing, but, as Stout himself notes in an afterward to the story, "a neat and original idea" underlies the motive for the crime. Purley Stebbins, on loan from the Wolfe series, merely serves to facilitate the exposition.

Eat, Drink, and Be Buried is a collection of short stories written by members of the Mystery Writers of America and edited by Stout. "By His Own Hand" originally appeared in *Manhunt* (April 1955).

84. "Justice Ends at Home"
in *Justice Ends at Home* (1977)

Detectives: Simon Leg—lawyer; Dan Culp—Leg's office boy.

Victim: Elaine Mount—errant wife; stabbed.

Client: William Mount—husband.

Other Principals: Judge Fraser Manton; Patrick Cummings—janitor.

Synopsis: Simon Leg is assigned the apparently hopeless task of defending William Mount. Dan Culp, convinced of Mount's innocence, energizes his employer's efforts. Culp locates a missing witness who, in a timely courtroom scene, discloses the murderer.

Comment: "Justice Ends at Home" is the title story of John McAleer's 1977 collection of sixteen of Stout's better pulp stories from the period 1912-1917. It originally appeared in *All-Story Weekly* on December 4, 1915. At sixty-three pages, it is the longest of the tales in the collection, and it is the one that most clearly anticipates his later career as a writer of detective fiction. As McAleer notes, Leg and Culp are *very* faint anticipations of Wolfe and Goodwin. Several of the other stories in the collection turn upon various criminal activities. All of them show Stout as, at the least, a competent writer at this early stage of his career. McAleer provides another useful critical introduction.

85. *Under the Andes* (1914, 1985)

Protagonists: Paul Lamar—sententious wealthy elder brother. Harry Lamar—impetuous wealthy younger brother. Desirée Le Mire—beautiful international adventuress.

Synopsis: Harry Lamar becomes infatuated with Desirée when she comes to New York. They elope to Denver, followed by the ever-protective Paul, who catches up with them at Pike's Peak. The threesome then proceed to San Francisco, charter a yacht, and sail to South America. They land at Callao, Peru, and, following a whim of Desirée, proceed inland to Cerro de Pasco, and thence up into the Andes. Entering a cave, they are precipitated into a lightless world of subterranean caverns, passages, streams, and lakes. This underground realm is inhabited by the descendants of the Incas driven from Huánuco by Hernando Pizarro in the sixteenth century. They have devolved into dark, hairy, four-foot-tall creatures who can see in the dark, but can no longer speak or hear. There follows a sequence of captivities and escapes in which the brothers massacre multitudes of the savages, and combat boneless reptilian monsters; and in which Desirée is briefly adored by the Incans and their king. The final escape is abetted by an earthquake; only two of the three protagonists return to New York.

Comment: John J. McAleer makes the best case for the narrative in his introduction to the 1985 reprint edition (the original story had been published in the February, 1914 issue of *All-Story*). It is not, however, hard to understand Stout's own disinclination to disinter the products of his first career as a popular writer between 1912 and 1916. *Under the Andes* is a competent adventure story, but the sequence of escapes, captivities, and massacres does not progress much, either in space or in drama. The contrast between the two brothers offers some interest, particularly in their relations with Desirée, but it has none of the roundedness of the contrast between Wolfe and Archie (or even that between minor characters in the better Wolfe stories). The underground Inca civilization possesses a few points of interest, but it seems chiefly to provide masses of corpses for the brothers to leave behind them in their various combats.

Perhaps the most intriguing moment in the novel comes on the last page, when the narrator seems to cast doubt on the reality of the entire preceding episode.

III.

NERO WOLFE and PERRY MASON:

From the Thirties to the Seventies

Erle Stanley Gardner launched Perry Mason's forty-year practice of criminal law in 1933; Rex Stout initiated Nero Wolfe's forty-one years of criminal investigation in 1934; but despite this remarkable correspondence of genre and chronology, the literary achievements of the two authors seem separated by more than the three thousand miles between Mason's Los Angeles and Wolfe's New York. Though both writers bound themselves to an unusually narrow set of formulas within the same conventional category of popular literature, the nature and the magnitude of their appeals to the common reader suggest their quite different approaches to the craft of mystery writing.

Erle Stanley Gardner was born in Massachusetts in 1889 and was raised in Northern California. He did not move to the Los Angeles area where most of his fiction is placed until 1911. Stout was born in Indiana in 1886, was raised in Kansas, and moved to the New York of Nero Wolfe in 1909. Prior to embarking on a career as a writer, Gardner had enjoyed considerable success as a lawyer and a businessman. He turned to writing in part to compensate for losses suffered in the Depression, and he served his apprenticeship by turning out hundreds of short stories for the pulp magazines. Stout's early success with his student banking plan, the Educational Thrift Service, was even more striking (and substantially more remunerative) than Gardner's legal career. He too was influenced by the Depression to take up writing, serving his apprenticeship through dozens (not hundreds) of submissions to the pulps. Both men were twice married. Gardner's first marriage ended in a thirty-year separation; Stout's first marriage ended in divorce. Both men were happily married a second time at the time of their deaths.

Gardner published the first Perry Mason novel, *The Case of the Velvet Claws*, in 1933, and followed it with eighty-four other Cases—eighty-one novels and three "novelettes"—the last one appearing in 1973, three years after Gardner's death. He also produced several subsidiary detective novel series, the two most important featuring the D.A. Doug Selby (nine novels, 1937-1949) and the detective firm of Bertha Cool and Donald Lam (twenty-nine novels, 1939-1970). Stout published *Fer-de-Lance*, the first Wolfe novel, in 1934; *A Family Affair*, the seventy-second Wolfe adventure (the thirty-third novel), appeared in 1975, the year of Stout's death. Despite several efforts, Stout never managed to match Gardner's facility in establishing secondary series. The three Tecumseh Fox novels (1939-1941) represent Nero Wolfe's most sustained competition.

Both writers chose to reside at a certain distance from the cities with which their fiction has identified them. Gardner carefully supervised the development of his ranch southeast of Los Angeles; Stout actually built his own house on an estate in Westchester County, New York. In their different ways, both men were active in social affairs, Gardner through his involvement with the Court of Last Resort and Stout through his commitment to a number of organizations and concerns—the American Civil Liberties Union, the War Writers Board, World Federalism, copyright reform. Here the temperamental and ideological differences begin to emerge. Stout is the eastern intellectual, sophisticated, *avant-garde*, engaged in political and sociological controversies. Gardner is the pragmatic westerner, concerned with concrete issues of basic human justice. Stout embraces causes; Gardner pleads cases. In the period during and following the Second World War, Stout displayed his skills as a polemicist on the radio and in print. Gardner's preferred weapon remained the legal brief. Stout employed wit, argument, and harangue to promote his views on the state of the nation and the world; Gardner compiled anecdotal records of miscarriages of justice. Stout sought legislative remedies; Gardner sought judicial reviews.

Almost inevitably, the two writers arrived at quite different notions of the form and function of a series of detective novels. Each of Perry Mason's cases comprises a self-contained fable in which the integrity, courage, and ingenuity of the defense lawyer triumphs over the confusion and the duplicity of witnesses and the misguidedness of prosecutors. Despite a proliferation of superficial complications, the fast-paced action rushes to its courtroom climax, and the moral drama remains unadulterated by psychological or socio-economic complexities. The sole question before the court is the identity of the murderer; all other issues are incompetent, irrelevant, and immaterial.

The Nero Wolfe novels are considerably less single-minded. The apportionment of innocence and guilt remains the paramount concern: Stout is not exempt from the requirement that every detective story end with a morally satisfying conclusion. But he is also willing to raise incidentally certain important issues which defy neat resolution within the action of the story itself. The world of Nero Wolfe includes crises which remain beyond the cure of detection. Wolfe often identifies culprits whom he cannot simply arrest: Nazis, Communists, capitalists, racists, the FBI, people who use "contact" as a verb. But by having Nero Wolfe detect and judge these social malefactors, Stout uses the infallible moral authority inherent in the figure of the Great Detective as a vehicle for propagating his own views on issues of social justice in the real world.

Gardner places Perry Mason outside of the history of his times; Stout just as deliberately places Nero Wolfe within it. Neither protagonist ages perceptibly during four decades of activity from the early thirties to the early seventies. But Perry Mason remains virtually untouched by depression, world war, and social unrest. Mason's Los Angeles is a utopia of homicide and legal procedure: only these verities apply. The only sign of changing times occurs when Mason, without comment, drops a dime instead of a nickel into the pay phone. By contrast, Nero Wolfe's career is clearly marked by the major events of the middle third of the twentieth century. Murders punctuate the record of his professional life, but his discourse covers larger matters. Perry Mason scans newspapers in search of headlines relating to his current case. Wolfe subscribes to the *New York Times,* and he studies every section. And current affairs—from Nazi espionage to Watergate—do impinge directly upon the action of his investigations. Wolfe's intellectual horizon is vastly larger than that of Perry Mason.

Wolfe's extensive acquaintance with the history of his times is accompanied by an unusually developed sense of his own personal history. The central characters of the Mason series—Mason, Della Street, and Paul Drake—have no definite pasts when they debut in 1933, and they acquire none over the next forty years. At the end of *The Case of the Velvet Claws,* Mason makes a point of consigning his client to oblivion. He shows her a drawer full of pasteboard folders.

> When I get all done with your case you're going to have a jacket in there, just about the same size as all of the other jackets, and it's going to be of just about the same importance. Miss Street is going to give you a number. Then if anything comes up, and I want to look back at the case to find out what was done, I'll give her that number, and she'll get me the jacket with the papers in it.

Nothing ever does come up; Mason never needs to look back at a case. He functions in a perpetual present, unrestrained by prior commitments or attachments.

Nero Wolfe is much more burdened by remembrance of things past. Each member of his household develops a character and a biography that extends beyond the requirements of plot. Midway through his career, in *The Black Mountain* (1954), Wolfe actually undertakes an expedition to Montenegro, recovering his roots as he guides Archie (and the reader) past his birthplace. And the Wolfe series is peopled with individuals who appear in more than one novel, often after a lapse of many years. These include friends and associates like Marko Vukcic, Lon Cohen, Dol Bonner, and Lily Rowan; clients like Paul Whipple; and even enemies like Arnold Zeck. Perry Mason's world begins anew with the arrival of each client; Wolfe's world accumulates meaning.

Perry Mason himself is more of an agent than a personality. Gardner never offers more than a minimalist portrait sufficient to identify his hero as a contemporary man: tall, dark, handsome, clad in a three-piece suit, and given to hooking his thumbs through the armholes of the vest as he paces around his office. Emerging from the *Black Mask* tradition, Mason's investigative method is the opposite of Wolfe's. He is an actor rather than a thinker, a boxer rather than a chess player. His technique depends upon constant motion and abrupt thrusts and counterthrusts In his first description of Mason, Gardner uses this image of the fighter: "a man who could work with infinite patience to jockey an adversary into just the right position, and then finish him with one terrific punch." Mason is essentially more a force—a protective energy—than he is a person. Psychological or ratiocinative complexities would only distract from his role as the vigorous and altruistic defender of the little guy.

The little guys (or, usually, the little gals) whom he defends all belong to the upwardly mobile middle class. The men are entrepreneurs, making their fortunes through honest or dishonest enterprise. The women are wives or widows or, most commonly, decent working girls looking forward to husbands and families. Nearly everyone (except the villain) is earnest, self-reliant, and, ultimately, triumphant. Gardner's optimistic common folk had an obvious appeal during the adversities of the thirties. That, relatively unaltered, they retained much of their appeal into the sixties and seventies demonstrates the persistence of the middle American dream.

The four non-detective novels Rex Stout published between 1929 and 1933 contain sophisticated portrayals of neurotic psychologies. A similar sophistication might be expected in the detective stories that followed. And indeed many of the characters in the early mysteries—both Wolfean and non-Wolfean—are memorably original. But characterization becomes increasingly perfunctory in the later novels. Wolfe encounters a lengthy procession of indistinguishable executives and heirs whose wealth provides them with an expedient autonomy and, in one way or another, provokes murder. Many of the later characters consist of little more than a name, a profession, a possible motive, and a lack of an alibi.

Yet as Wolfe's upper class clientele grows more hollow, Wolfe himself grows more solid. A collage of eccentricities evolves into an impressive character, a Great Cham of Detection. Archie Goodwin may seem closer in type to Perry Mason. Active, resilient, irreverent—he too has hardboiled genes in his chromosomes. But the texture of Archie's life is far more tangible than that of Perry Mason; through his distinctive voice, he too emerges as a rounded figure.

The facility with which Erle Stanley Gardner manufactured mystery plots is legend. The Mason novels include concealed motives, disconcerting revelations, recalcitrant or elusive witnesses, and always a sound presentation of legal and forensic technicalities. The action is fast-paced and unrelenting. The Mason novels necessarily generate two coherent, competing plots: a false plot fabricated by the killer and promoted by the prosecutor, and a true plot uncovered through the clever cross-examinations of the defense attorney. The construction of these superimposed plots sometimes taxes even Gardner's ingenuity, but at their best, Gardner's novels create the satisfying illusion that though the web of circumstances be a tangled one indeed, an aggressive dialectician like Perry Mason can untie the knots and reveal the simple, absolute lines of innocence and guilt.

Rex Stout's plotting has rarely won high praise. The absence of a dominant protagonist compelled him to devote more attention to managing the action of the non-Wolfe narratives, and as a result these comprise some of his better mysteries. The early Wolfe novels also develop some imaginative predicaments, but most of the later Wolfe novels and novellas seem rather cavalier in the matter of plot. The routine of gathering the principal characters in Wolfe's office becomes an almost empty formality. On occasion Wolfe declines even to pretend that he has profited from the exercise. His invariable success at bludgeoning the principals into attending these convocations (or at bludgeoning Inspector Cramer into compelling them to attend) also becomes too predictable. Finally, Wolfe all too often identifies the criminal not through inference and analysis, but through the execution of an unconvincing stratagem which prompts the guilty individual to confess or otherwise to manifest his or her guilt. These substantial defects, added to the virtual universality of motive and opportunity in any given tale, insure that plot will never be the chief appeal of Stout's fiction.

Neither Gardner nor Stout pays much attention to the environment of crime. One need only compare Gardner's depiction of Los Angeles to that of Raymond Chandler or Ross Macdonald to confirm that his interest clearly lies elsewhere. Similarly, Stout's New York City has none of the heightened atmosphere of Mickey Spillane's, none of the verisimilitude of Ed McBain's depiction of the city. Gardner's city consists principally of streets; Stout's of well-appointed mid-town offices and penthouses. Perry Mason makes frequent stops at motels, hotels, middle-class apartment buildings, and single-family dwellings, but the narrative notices only those details which have a bearing on the business at hand. As narrator of the Wolfe stories, Archie Goodwin has more license to respond to nonessential detail, but eventually one Manhattan high-rise begins to resemble the next; one Westchester County estate becomes indistinguishable from any other.

Stout holds an obvious advantage over Gardner in the realization of the detective's personal territory. Perry Mason's office is defined in terms of functional items such as doors and rooms; the reader must be able to follow the characters' moves as they enter and exit, wait and consult. And the only certain features of Mason's apartment are a bed and a telephone. By contrast, Wolfe's brownstone on West Thirty-Fifth Street ranks second only to 221B Baker Street in the interest of its layout and its furnishings. Here is a place that is tangible, familiar, and comfortable; this setting is one of the chief virtues of Stout's detective series.

Stout may also claim the advantage in the matter of style, though the merit of Gardner's pedestrian prose should not be underrated. Gardner's style is serviceable in the best sense of the world. It never interferes with the pace of the story; it is brilliantly and seductively banal. Gardner relies upon very short paragraphs, and wherever possible, he uses dialogue to advance the narrative—expository dialogue of the sort never spoken by man, yet dialogue which easily and economically communicates the pertinent information required to carry the plot forward. Raymond Chandler intended no compliment when he compared Gardner's prose to the loud monotone of a French taxi horn, but like a taxi horn, Gardner's prose does clear the way for the onrush of action.

The Nero Wolfe novels combine two very attractive styles: the fluid, wise-cracking narrative of Archie Goodwin and the imperial, aphoristic interjections of Nero Wolfe. Archie has learned his vernacular rhetoric at the heels of such masters as Race Williams and the Continental Op, but he leavens their cynicism with his boyish enthusiasm. Nero Wolfe may have absorbed the lessons of the epigrammatic Holmes and the magisterial Dr. Thorndyke, but the neoclassical decorum of his syntax and diction mark him as an original. Once again, Archie's freshness and Wolfe's authority seem to diminish somewhat with time, but even in the late novels, the collision between their two styles makes for enjoyable reading.

Rex Stout's popularity never approached that of Erle Stanley Gardner. By 1965 seventy-five of Gardner's novels had sold more than a million copies; none of Stout's books had reached this landmark. Alice Payne Hackett's and James Henry Durke's list of the fifty-five best-selling novels in the category of crime and suspense, 1895-1975, included twenty-five of

Gardner's books, none of Stout's. Yet, equally clearly, Stout is the greater writer, highly regarded by students of popular literature, and by other writers as well. In his biography of Stout, John McAleer was able to cite commendations not only from Stout's fellow mystery writers James M. Cain, Nicholas Freeling, Ross Macdonald, Georges Simenon, Julian Symons—but also from "major" contemporary authors: Graham Greene, J. B. Priestley, Gilbert Highet, Kingsley Amis, E. B. White. The contrast between the two appeals—Gardner's low brow and Stout's upper middle brow—lies in each author's different approaches to their narratives.

For both Perry Mason and Nero Wolfe, language is the principal instrument for uncovering moral reality. Both investigators rely upon questions, not microscopes; truth emerges through interviews and cross-examinations and interviews, not through precise measurements and police procedures. The essential difference between the mobile lawyer and the stationary detective appears in Mason's assumption that uncovering morality is the only function of language. Action, not description, is real; and through action Mason solves crimes. In the world of Nero Wolfe, language is reality; it is an end as well as a means. It creates Wolfe's world, and through his mastery of it—of the logos—Wolfe can control his world. Nero Wolfe is simply unimaginable in any medium other than the words of Archie Goodwin. Gardner's more utilitarian view of language explains why Perry Mason could survive intact when transferred to the visual media of film and television. Images merely replace description. The subjective impressions and interpretations implied in the language of Wolfe and Archie cannot be as easily conveyed in images, and so their transition to film was notably less successful.

This is not to suggest that Gardner's prose was naively transparent or that Stout's involved Jamesian nuances. Both authors were engaged in reproducing formular moral fables. But Gardner achieved his phenomenal popularity by avoiding all complexities. Motives and actions in his fiction may be complicated, but they are never ambiguous. Gardner's avoidance of any sense of time or place locates Mason's unsubstantial world in the neighborhood of Aesop's simplified realm of hares and tortoises. Gardner's aesthetic is as reductive as his ethic: mimesis and morality are equally in a plain style. And in this respect, his work is perhaps more coherent that Stout's. In the world of Nero Wolfe Rex Stout attempts to join artful language with simplistic, generic morality. At its best, his fiction manages to establish that certain fundamental categories of innocence and guilt underlie a richly perceived fabric of social relations. The texture of life is sophisticated, but the basic rules of behavior are unambivalent.

James Russell Lowell appraised the achievement of James Fenimore Cooper by acknowledging the originality of Natty Bumppo:

The men who have given to one character life
And objective existence are not very rife;
You may number them all, both prose-writers
    and singers
Without overrunning the bounds of your fingers.
—*A Fable for Critics*

Within the limits of the genre, the same may be said of Rex Stout: no other detectives are more alive than Nero Wolfe and Archie Goodwin. It cannot be said that Erle Stanley Gardner ever really gives life to Perry Mason. Mason is as stereotypical as his clients, his secretary, his city. But the stereotype evidently had an archetypal resonance for midcentury Americans. Nero Wolfe entered the pantheon of Great Detectives; Perry Mason entered the common vocabulary.

IV.

FAMILY, the HERON, and SENATOR McCARTHY:

Aspects of Rex Stout's Originality

Debuting in 1934, Nero Wolfe appeared at the moment when the detective story was in its most polarized state, with the Golden Age novelists claiming the legitimate, direct descent from Dupin and Holmes for their country house crimes, and the Hard-boiled novelists acknowledging a more sinister, wrong-side-of-the-sheets heritage for their mean streets murders. Rex Stout, famously, sought to unite the appeals of both poles, with Wolfe playing the role of the eccentric, ratiocinative Great Detective, and Archie Goodwin assuming the guise of the smart aleck tough-guy. The friction between the two types was, from the beginning, a source of the series' appeal; both Stout and his readers realized that it enabled him to take neither version of detective too seriously. But if the two types of detective could entertainingly cohabit a New York City brownstone, they could do so only in one type of world: the New York City of Wolfe and Goodwin had to be either what W.H. Auden called a Great Good Place, in the tradition of Poirot and Lord Peter Wimsey and Philo Vance; or a Great Wrong Place, in the tradition of Race Williams, Sam Spade, and the Continental Op. Either it would be an enclosed, safe world with a fixed cast of suspects, one of whom was cleverly concealing his guilt; or it would be an open and violent world, where men with guns (and dames with gams) kept knocking on the door.

Stout chose the Great Good Place. Wolfe and Goodwin find their cases in safe, insulated interiors—the homes and offices of the wealthy, places where the odd footprint or the peculiar tear in the evening gown may be significant indeed, but where what happens outside the walls can be ignored as irrelevant. Despite Archie Goodwin's semi-tough talk and occasional semi-tough action, we are, from Wolfe's first case, *Fer-de-Lance* (1934) to his last, *A Family Affair* (1975), in Great Good Places. The murder scenes are clean and well-lighted; the corpses are an affront to the prevailing decent order. The first murder that Wolfe investigates takes place on the manicured fairway of an exclusive country club; most of the rest take place in non-rent-controlled habitations. As in most classical mysteries, the specific setting may be described in concrete detail—the furniture cataloged, the meal itemized, the comings and goings of the suspects carefully tabulated, but the social environment of the larger urban scene is ignored. Neither Wolfe nor Archie shows much knowledge of or interest in ethnic New York—in Harlem, or Chinatown or the Lower East Side, or any part of outer four boroughs other than the stadiums of the Bronx and Queens. The Great Good Places of the Golden Age are always scenes of Arcadian innocence, where the rhythms of life reflect a natural order—a conspicuous order which the murder disrupts. That is the point of placing the body in the library, or in the resort hotel, or even in a carefully regulated carriage of the Orient Express. It is an offense to the nature of the Great Good Place, an intrusion of an alien evil.

Order is clearly the rule in Wolfe's world; certainly in his private world of the brownstone on West 35th Street, where he so inflexibly applies the routines for which he is famous—plant rooms between 9:00 and 11:00 and between 4:00 and 6:00; no business discussed at meals. The rooftop orchids are the clearest sign that the brownstone represents an eccentric, self-willed Arcadia in the midst of Manhattan. It is a retreat. And Wolfe's clients are predominately Manhattan townhouse owners, or spouses of townhouse owners or children of townhouse owners, or people who, if they lived in Manhattan, would own townhouses; they appeal to him because their own Great Good Places have been invaded by disorder of the worst sort. Wolfe's mission, then, is to re-order their world, to recover within their walls the order that he maintains in his own.

No one expects him to bring order to the mean streets in between. Wolfe himself will not even step foot upon the street except under the greatest duress. The streets of Wolfe's world are, indeed, unreal. This unreality is epitomized in the vehicle which Wolfe uses to navigate them. When Archie Goodwin does drive the avenues of New York, he does so not in a Plymouth, or a Chevy, or even in a Lincoln or a Mercedes; he drives a "Heron." No real New Yorker drives a Heron; no one drives a Heron; there are no Herons.

But if in these respects Stout located his detective in a timeless Arcadian nowhereland, in two important respects he went beyond the Golden Age paradigm of the Great Good Place, and in one of these, he was foreshadowed a major development in the genre. Stout's first anti-Classical move lay in giving his detective a family. The standard model Classical detective, from Poe to Conan Doyle to Christie to Van Dine to Queen, was a bachelor, and, aside from a intimate comrade or two, an isolated bachelor. Wolfe too is a bachelor, but Stout gave him a family—a literal family with the introduction of an adopted daughter in *Over My Dead Body* (1940), but, more importantly, an irregular family that included Archie Goodwin, Fritz Brenner, and Theodore Horstmann; Inspector Cramer and Sergeant Stebbins; Saul Panzer, Orrie Cather, Fred Durkin, Johnny Keems, and Bill Gore; Marko Vukcic, Doc Vollmer, Nathaniel Parker and Lon Cohen. Some of these are functional fixtures, with little more depth of character than a Paul Drake or Della Street. But three of them die in the course of the Wolfe saga, and their deaths—especially those of Vukcic and Cather—are emotionally significant events in Wolfe's life. And this means that Wolfe has an emotional life; he has ties to other people—complicated, human ties. The only major detective who exceeded Wolfe in this regard was Dorothy Sayers' Lord Peter Wimsey, who developed such a remarkable inner life that he became a lover as well as a detective. But in becoming a lover—and then a husband, and finally even a father—Wimsey rendered himself ineligible as a detective.

Wolfe remained eligible. Rex Stout never went as far as Dorothy Sayers did in giving his detective a heart, but he did increasingly emphasize the evolution of Wolfe's extended household as a main point of interest in the series. Archie's affair with Lily Rowan is shallow when compared to that between Peter Wimsey and Harriet Vane, but it does go on and on: Archie meets her in *Some Buried Caesar* (1939) and their affair continues without developing very much through the remainder of the series. Stronger examples of Stout's use of family elements occur as Wolfe and his supporting cast experience drastic changes in their lives: in 1940, Wolfe suddenly rediscovers his adopted Croatian daughter (*Over My Dead Body*); she will only appear in one other novel, but suddenly recovered, long-lost daughters were not, in the 1940s, a staple of the genre. During the Second World War, Wolfe adheres strictly to rationing, while his family fight the war: Archie works for Army Intelligence, and Saul Panzer, Fred Durkin, Orrie Cather, and Johnny Keems all serve overseas ("Help Wanted, Male"). In the three Zeck novels (1948-50), Wolfe faces an extended engagement with a single criminal mastermind, and is compelled to abandon his home; this crisis (unlike Sherlock Holmes's famous hiatus) is used to develop both Wolfe and Goodwin as characters and as comrades. In *The Black Mountain* (1954), Wolfe's adopted daughter and his best friend, Marko Vukcic, who had appeared in a minor role in half a dozen novels, are both killed, and in pursuit of his investigation, Wolfe revisits his Montenegrin homeland. Montenegrin roots—roots of any kind—were not attributes bestowed on detectives. In *Might As Well Be Dead* (1956), one of Wolfe's team of supporting detectives is killed; and, most famously, in the final Wolfe novel with the significant title, *A Family Affair* (1975), another of the supporting detectives turns out to be the killer in the case under investigation. In all of these instances,

Wolfe ceases to be the purely aloof intellect which detectives such as Philo Vance, Ellery Queen, and Hercule Poirot claimed to be. He engages in significant personal relationships.

Wolfe remains predominantly the isolated, eccentric genius. But emotional currents do wash through the brownstone, and they become a major source of interest, as the interplay between Wolfe and his friends and his employees and his adoptive relations shift and change. Wolfe may occupy the stable, unmoving center; but around him flow a variety of evolving characters, and Wolfe himself is not entirely untouched. Detectives since the 1970s have engaged in such an extensive set of human relationships, acquiring and losing and often re-acquiring spouses and friends and lovers and children, that the novelty of Nero Wolfe's family life may be overlooked.

Rex Stout's greater innovation lay in his attention to the realities of the larger world. Nero Wolfe might not know the streets of his city very well, but he knew his nation. There are, for example, references in *Fer-de-Lance* to national issues such as Prohibition, and the Depression, and the Lindbergh baby. A few other writers of Golden Age detective stories were inserting a few topical references of this sort, but none to the degree Stout did. The Wolfe series is probably the only major detective story series before the 1970s to make national affairs an essential part of the detective's world, and few of the post-1970 series are as explicit about historical events and figures. Philip Marlowe never notices Pearl Harbor, or the Japanese internments, or the atom bomb. Marlowe notices that Los Angeles has the personality of a paper cup, but does not observe that Senator McCarthy has made an American era his own. Nero Wolfe and Archie Goodwin lack the sharpness to notice what sort of cup New York City might be, but they do notice the junior senator from Wisconsin and his impact on America. They live in their time; they notice and judge its events. Stout does not feel obligated to invent a surrogate senator from a vaguely Midwestern state; Nero Wolfe despises Joseph R. McCarthy, and he says so. Archie may drive a Heron, but when it comes to J. Edgar Hoover or Richard M. Nixon, he names names.

This indulgence in direct commentary upon contemporary political issues is there from the beginning, but it increases as the series moves into the 1940s and 1950s. In 1936, Wolfe and Goodwin comment upon Jews and Fascism and Communism; in 1938 they debate race relations in America as a major side issue in an investigation; in 1940 Nero Wolfe acknowledges that he has contributed to the anti-fascist cause in Spain; in 1944, Archie serves in military intelligence, and Wolfe vows to learn to kill Germans; in 1946, Wolfe allows his bias against predatory capitalism to guide the manner in which he solves a crime; in 1949, Archie informs us that in support of Henry Wallace, Wolfe investigated a case involving Communist subversion; Wolfe acts again against Communism in 1952, though he also disparages McCarthyite red-baiting; in 1964 Wolfe returns to the topic of race relations in America, with the Civil Rights movement becoming a central issue in an investigation; in 1965, Wolfe sets himself in deliberate and direct opposition to the arrogance of J. Edgar Hoover and his FBI; in 1969 he comments upon the Vietnam War, the protests in Berkeley, California, and Alexander Solzhenitzyn; in 1973 upon issues of feminism and the Arab-Israeli conflict; and in 1975 upon Watergate.

Although Wolfe and Goodwin undertake to detect only those crimes committed by a homogeneous clientele of Great Good Placers, from their fixed point on West 35th Street they also observe the turning world of national and global political culture. And they use the moral authority, which they acquire in infallibly solving townhouse homicides to give weight to their judgments upon current events. By an easily managed transference, Nero Wolfe's magisterial ability to bring order to very artificial Great Good Places gives a credibility to his magisterial pronouncements on fascism or red-baiting or feminism in the real world beyond his brownstone, and beyond the island of Manhattan. Because we know that he is always right about whodunit, we are persuaded he is also right about Senator McCarthy, Director Hoover, and President Nixon.

Especially after 1970, detective story writers would adopt this trick which Stout pioneered; explicit social and political commentary, naming names, becomes increasingly common as detectives are set in their historical moments. Indeed, the commentary appears often to be the *raison d'être*: for many post-70s writers, the agenda is primary, and the entertainment is for marketing purposes. They write because they have something to say about racism, feminism, sexual orientationism, whatever, and the formulas of the genre are the spoonful of sugar. Rex Stout would probably have been appalled by some of the political correctness of the commentary, but he would, I think, have applauded the development. Mere polemic-with-a-murder is a dull thing, but many of the polemicists are, in fact, clever writers. Not quite as clever as Wolfe and Archie, true; but who is?

BIBLIOGRAPHY

1. The Nero Wolfe Books

Rex Stout's publishers included: Vanguard Press (1929-31), Farrar and Rinehart (1933-44), Viking Press (1946-77), and Bantam Books (1985).

Fer-de-Lance. 1934, 313 p.
The League of Frightened Men. 1935, 308 p.
The Rubber Band. 1936, 302 p.
The Red Box. 1937, 298 p.
Too Many Cooks. 1938, 303 p.
Some Buried Caesar. 1939, 296 p.
Over My Dead Body. 1940, 293 p.
Where There's a Will. 1940, 272 p.
Black Orchids. 1942, 271 p.
Not Quite Dead Enough. 1944, 220 p.
The Silent Speaker. 1946, 308 p.
Too Many Women. 1947, 251 p.
And Be a Villain. 1948, 216 p.
Trouble in Triplicate. 1949, 186 p.
The Second Confession. 1949, 245 p.
Three Doors to Death. 1950, 244 p.
In the Best Families. 1950, 246 p.
Curtains for Three. 1951, 247 p.
Murder by the Book. 1951, 248 p.
Triple Jeopardy. 1952, 216 p.
Prisoner's Base. 1952, 186 p.
The Golden Spiders. 1953, 186 p.
Three Men Out. 1954, 181 p.
The Black Mountain. 1954, 183 p.
Before Midnight. 1955, 184 p.
Three Witnesses. 1956, 185 p.
Might As Well Be Dead. 1956, 186 p.
Three for the Chair. 1957, 183 p.
If Death Ever Slept. 1957, 186 p.
And Four to Go. 1958, 190 p.
Champagne for One. 1958, 184 p.
Plot It Yourself. 1959, 183 p.
Three at Wolfe's Door. 1960, 186 p.
Too Many Clients. 1960, 183 p.
The Final Deduction. 1961, 182 p.
Homicide Trinity. 1962, 182 p.

Gambit. 1962, 188 p.

The Mother Hunt. 1963, 182 p.

Trio for Blunt Instruments. 1964, 247 p.

A Right to Die. 1964, 182 p.

The Doorbell Rang. 1965, 186 p.

Death of a Doxy. 1966, 186 p.

The Father Hunt. 1968, 184 p.

Death of a Dude. 1969, 182 p.

Please Pass the Guilt. 1973, 150 p.

A Family Affair. 1975, 152 p.

Corsage. (James A. Rock & Co., Pubs.) 1977, 180 p.

Death Times Three. 1985, 213 p.

2. Other Mysteries

The President Vanishes. 1934, 296 p.

The Hand in the Glove. 1937, 284 p.

Mountain Cat. 1939, 306 p.

Double for Death. 1939, 284 p.

Red Threads, in *The Mystery Book.* 1939, [255] p.

Bad for Business, in *The Second Mystery Books.* 1940, [204] p.

The Broken Vase. 1941, 275 p.

Alphabet Hicks. 1941, 271 p.

"Tough Cop's Gift." *What's New; Special Christmas Edition.* Abbott
   Laboratories, 1953. (Alternate titles: "Cop's Gift," "Nobody Deserved
   Justice," and "Santa Claus Beat.")

Justice Ends at Home. 1977, 267 p.

3. Mainstream Novels and Others

How Like a God. 1929, 313 p.

Seed on the Wind. 1930, 310 p.

Golden Remedy. 1931, 292 p.

Forest Fire. 1933, 305 p.

O Careless Love! 1935, 272 p.

Mr. Cinderella. 1938, 275 p.

The Illustrious Dunderheads, edited by Rex Stout. Alfred A. Knopf, 1942,
   192 p.

Rue Morgue No. 1, edited by Rex Stout and Louis Greenfield. Creative Age
   Press, 1946, 403 p.

Eat, Drink, and Be Buried, edited by Rex Stout. Viking, 1956, 246 p.

The Nero Wolfe Cook Book, edited by Rex Stout. Viking, 1973, 203 p.

Under the Andes. Penzler Books, 1985, 286 p. Fantasy adventure.

4. Authorized Pastiches by Robert Goldsborough

Murder in E Minor. Bantam, 1986.
Death on Deadline. Bantam, 1987.
Bloodied Ivy. Bantam, 1988.
The Last Coincidence. Bantam, 1989.
Fade to Black. Bantam, 1990.
Silver Spire. Bantam, 1992.
Missing Chapter. Bantam, 1994.

5. Secondary Sources

Stout had the good fortune to acquire John McAleer as his biographer. As a result, Stout's intellectually eventful life has been well-covered in *Rex Stout: A Biography.*

Nearly thirty years after his death, Stout's fiction has remained popular, both in print and on video. It has fared somewhat less well in the academy. Scholars appear to undervalue his achievement. David R. Anderson provides a good introduction to the fiction in Rex Stout (1984), but it is clear that Stout has received less attention than many of his peers. The *MLA Bibliography*, for example, includes 17 citations of works on Rex Stout's fiction since 1963 (and eight of these are articles from *Armchair Detective*). Raymond Chandler, by contrast, claims 253 citations for the same period, Dashiell Hammett 175, Ross Macdonald 86, Agatha Christie 139, Dorothy Sayers 41, Georges Simenon 136. (On the other hand, Stout's hugely popular contemporary, Erle Stanley Gardner, receives only 13.) In the end, Stout's achievement speaks for itself: the Nero Wolfe series constitutes a landmark in the history of detective fiction.

Anderson, David R. "Crime and Character: Notes on Rex Stout's Early Fiction." *Armchair Detective* 13 (1980): 169-72.
_____. *Rex Stout.* New York: Frederick Ungar, 1984.
_____. "Rex Stout." *Mystery and Suspense Writers.* Ed. Robin Winks and Maureen Corrigan. Vol 2. New York: Scribner's, 1998.
Baring-Gould, William S. *Nero Wolfe of West Thirty-Fifth Street.* New York: Viking, 1969.
Barzun, Jacques. *A Birthday Tribute to Rex Stout.* New York: Viking 1965.
Beiderwell, Bruce. "State Power and Self-Destruction: Rex Stout and the Romance of Justice." *Journal of Popular Culture* 27.1 (Summer 1993): 13-22.
Darby, Ken. *The Brownstone House of Nero Wolfe.* Boston: Little, Brown, 1983.
Dunlap, Thomas Paine. "Nero Wolfe and Seven Pillars." *T.E. Notes* 4.8 (Oct 1993): 7-8.

Edel, Leon. "The Figure Under the Carpet." *Telling Lives: The Biographer's Art.* Ed. March Pachter. Washington: New Republic Books, 1979.

Gerhardt, Mia I. "'Homicide West': Some Observations on the Nero Wolfe Stories of Rex Stout." *English Studies* 49 (1968): 107-127.

Gotwald, Frederick G. *The Nero Wolfe Handbook.* Salisbury, NC, 2000 (Revised).

Isaac, Frederick. "Enter the Fat Man: Rex Stout's *Fer-de-Lance.*" *In the Beginning: First Novels in Mystery Series.*" Ed. Mary Jean DeMarr. Bowling Green: Popular Press, 1995.

Kagan, Donald and Walter A. Ralls. "A Wolfe in Stout Clothing." *Armchair Detective* 28.2 (Spring 1995): 176-83.

Knight, Arthur. "An Appreciation of Archie Goodwin." *Armchair Detective 12* (1979): 328-29.

McAleer, John. "Rex Stout Newsletter." *Armchair Detective* 11 (1978): 257.

_____. *Rex Stout: A Biography.* Boston: Little, Brown, 1977;

_____. *Rex Stout: A Biography.* (Millennial Edition) Rockville, MD: James A. Rock & Co., Pubs., 2002;

_____. *Royal Decree: Conversations with Rex Stout.* Ashton, MD: Pontes Press, 1983.

Nickerson, Edward A. "'Realistic' Crime Fiction: An Anatomy of Evil People." *The Centenial Review* 25.2 (Spring 1981): 101-32.

Penzler, Otto. "Collecting Mystery Fiction: Rex Stout." Three parts: *Armchair Detective* 29.3 (Summer 1996): 302-06; 29.4 (Fall 1996): 418-29; 30.1 (Winter 1997): 35-38. See also 23.3 (Summer 1990): 314-17.

Rauber, D. F. "Sherlock Holmes and Nero Wolfe: The Role of the 'Great Detective' in Intellectual History." *Journal of Popular Culture* 6 (Spring 1973): 483-95.

Rife, David. "Rex Stout and William Faulkner's Nobel Prize Speech." *Journal of Modern Literature* 10.1 (March 1983): 151-2.

Seigel, Jeff. "A Few Thoughts about Nero Wolfe." *Mystery Scene* 54 (1996): 22-23.

Stafford, Norman E. "Partners in Crime." *Armchair Detective* 23.3 (Summer 1990): 349-53.

Symons, Julian. "In Which Archie Goodwin Remembers." *The Great Detectives.* New York: Harry N. Abrams, 1981.

Townsend, Guy M. "The Nero Wolfe Saga." *Mystery Fancier* 2.1–4.3 (1978-80) (serialized in 19 parts)

Townsend, Guy, M. and John McAleer. *Rex Stout: An Annotated Primary and Secondary Bibliography.* New York: Garland, 1980.

6. Additional Periodical Commentary

Best Sellers: 1 November 1973; *Holiday*: November 1969; *National Review*: 12 August 2002: 51 (review of A & E series by Terry Teachout); *Newsweek*: 22 March 1971; *New Republic*: 30 July 1977: 41-43; *New York Herald Tribune*: 10 October 1965; *New York Times Book Review*: 30 June 1968; 14 July 1968; 11 November 1973; *New Yorker*: 14 October 1944: 73-75 (comments of Edmund Wilson); *Publisher's Weekly*: 29 October 1973; *Time*: 21 March 1969; *Washington Post*: 5 October 1969

ADAPTATIONS

Film

Meet Nero Wolfe (1936). Directed by Herbert J. Biberman, with Edward Arnold (Wolfe) and Lionel Stander (Goodwin). Based on *Fer de Lance*, with Rita Hayworth as Maria Maringola (= Maria Maffei).

The League of Frightened Men (1937). Directed by Alfred E. Green, with Walter Connolly (Wolfe), Lionel Stander (Goodwin).

The President Vanishes (1934). Directed by William A. Wellman, with Edward Arnold (Lewis Wardell), Arthur Byron (President Stanley Craig), Paul Kelly (Chick Moffat), and with Rosalind Russell as Sally Voorman. UK title: *Strange Conspiracy*.

Television

Nero Wolfe (1979). Directed by Frank D. Gilroy, with Thayer David (Wolfe), Tom Mason (Goodwin). The two-hour pilot was based on *The Doorbell Rang* and aired on ABC on 18 December 1979

Nero Wolfe (1981). With William Conrad (Wolfe), Lee Horsley (Goodwin). Thirteen one-hour episodes aired from 16 January to 25 August on NBC.

Lady Against the Odds (1992). Directed by Bradford May, with Crystal Bernard (Bonner). Based on *The Hand in the Glove*.

The A & E Television Series

The directors include Bill Duke, Timothy Hutton, Neill Fearnley, Holly Dale. With Maury Chaykin (Wolfe), Timothy Hutton (Goodwin), Colin Fox (Brenner), Bill Smitrovich (Cramer), Conrad Dunn (Panzer)

Golden Spiders (5 March 2000)
The Doorbell Rang (22 April 2001)
Champagne for One (29 April and 6 May 2001)

Prisoner's Base (13 and 20 May 2001)
Eeny Meeny Murder Mo (3 June 2001)
Disguise for Murder (17 June 2001)
Door to Death (24 June 2001)
Christmas Party (1 July 2001)
Over My Dead Body (8 and 15 July 2001)
Death of a Doxy (14 April 2002)
The Next Witness (21 April 2002)
Die Like a Dog (28 April 2002)
Murder is Corny (5 May 2002)
The Mother Hunt (12 and 19 May 2002)
Poison à la Carte (26 May 2002)
Too Many Clients (2 and 9 June 2002)
Before I Die (16 June 2002)
Help Wanted, Male (30 June 2002)
The Silent Speaker (14 and 21 July 2002)
Cop Killer (11 Aug 2002)
Immune to Murder (18 Aug 2002)

Other Television Adaptations

Too Many Cooks was filmed for German television as *Zu viele Köchen* (1961)

Seven Nero Wolfe movies were filmed for Italian television: *Veleno in sartoria* (1969), *Un incidente di caccia* (1969), *La cas degli attori* (1969), *Il pesce più grosso* (1969), *Sfida al Cioccolato* (1970), *La bella bugiarda* (1971), *Salsicce 'Mezzanotte'* (1971)

Radio

The Adventures of Nero Wolfe. 1943-44, NBC Blue, with Santos Ortega (Wolfe) (replaced by Luis Van Rooten in 1944) and John Gibson (Goodwin). The series aired from 5 July 1943 to 14 July 1944.

The Adventures of Nero Wolfe. 1945-46, MBS, with Francis X Bushman (Wolfe) and Elliott Lewis (Goodwin).

New Adventures of Nero Wolfe. 1950, NBC, with Sydney Greenstreet (Wolfe). Gerald Mohr, Wally Maher, Harry Bartell, Herb Ellis, Lawrence Dobkin, and others played Goodwin. The series aired from 20 October 1950 to 27 April 1951.

INDEX

About J. Kenneth Van Dover

J. K. Van Dover is Professor of English at Lincoln University (Pennsylvania). He has taught American Literature (including the detective story) at the University of Tübingen and the University of Stuttgart in Germany, and at Nankai University in China. He is the author of a number of studies of detective fiction, including *Murder in the Millions: Erle Stanley Gardner, Mickey Spillane, and Ian Fleming; Polemical Pulps: The Novels of Sjöwall and Wahlöö; You Know My Method: The Science of the Detective;* and, with John Jebb, *Isn't Justice Always Unfair? The Detective in Southern Literature.*

REX STOUT: A Majesty's Life
by John McAleer

An Edgar Award Winning Biography

Almost twenty-five years ago, the original jacket notes for John McAleer's *Rex Stout: A Biography*, reborn here in a new millennial edition as *Rex Stout: A Majesty's Life*, stated that it was "a splendid biography" for current fans and "future members of the 'Wolfe pack.'" Over two decades later, the "Wolfe pack" includes literally millions of fans, both old and new.

The first edition of *Rex Stout: A Biography* won the 1978 Mystery Writers of America's coveted "Edgar" award as Best Critical or Biographical Work. This new edition of John McAleer's classic biography will be a welcome treat for readers.

Renamed for the new millennium and enhanced with additional photographs, a new introduction by John McAleer and a nostalgic look at Rex Stout's "High Meadow" in an afterword by Andrew McAleer (the author's son who visited the estate at the age of eleven), *Rex Stout: A Majesty's Life* will captivate readers with the story of this remarkable man.

John McAleer's biography, written with the passion of the fan and the discipline of the scholar, and with the gracious and intimate participation of Rex himself, is an acknowledged masterpiece of American biographical writing. It is a remarkable vindication of the sentiment expressed in John Ruskin's oft-quoted but rarely realized aphorism: "When love and skill work together, expect a masterpiece." 6x9, 668 pages, photos.
Paperback, ISBN 0-918736-44-7, $26.95
Hardcover, ISBN 0-918736-43-9, $44.95

An Informal Interview with Rex Stout by Michael Bourne

Over one hour with Stout on life, writing, Nero Wolfe and Archie Goodwin. Conducted in April 1973 by Michael Bourne, editor of the

limited edition (and long out-of-print) *Corsage: A Bouquet of Rex Stout and Nero Wolfe* at Rex Stout's home at High Meadow. Makes a great gift. Early orders will still receive copies of the original limited release of 276 numbered copies with special packaging.

Audio Cassette, 70+ minutes, ISBN 0-918736-44-7
$20.00 (includes shipping) *Order direct from publisher.*

The Yellowback Mystery Series

Arsène Lupin versus Holmlock Shears
by Maurice Leblanc

Arsène Lupin, the "Gentleman Burglar" of France, appeared from the pen of Maurice Leblanc (1864–1941) in 1905. In the words of a prominent critic, Leblanc brought to the character "the skill of Sherlock Holmes, the resourcefulness of Raffles, the refinement of a casuist, the epigrammatic nimbleness of La Rouchefoucauld and the gallantry of Du Guesclin."

Paper $16.95, ISBN 0-918736-12-9   Hardcover $26.95, ISBN 0-918736-11-0

The Dorrington Deed-Box
by Arthur Morrison

Arthur Morrison (1863–1945) is best remembered in the mystery field for his casebook stories (à la Conan Doyle) of the detective "Martin Hewitt" (1896). Less well-known, but far more groundbreaking, was *The Dorrington Deed-Box*, in which he chronicles the exploits of Horace Dorrington, a raconteur and scoundrel who hails from a very different social strata than the typical Victorian detective. Dorrington, an anti-hero before his time, is as likely to pre-empt a criminal plot as he is to solve it.

Paper $16.95, ISBN 0-918736-14-5   Hardcover $26.95, ISBN 0-918736-13-7

An African Millionaire
by Grant Allen

Grant Allen (1848–1899) was one of the most prolific writers of the Victorian era. Allen's most enduring character, however, is "Colonel Clay," the gentleman rogue and thief who steals from the corrupt "African millionaire," a victim who is repeatedly led astray by the clever Colonel while fueled by his own greed. A delightful early entry in the British "rogue" gallery of gentlemen crooks, appearing two years before the introduction of E. W. Hornung's famous fictional rogue, "Raffles."

Paper $16.95: ISBN 0-918736-16-1   Hardcover $26.95: ISBN 0-918736-15-3

James A. Rock & Company, Publishers
9710 Traville Gateway Drive, Box 305
Rockville, Maryland 20850

*Most titles are available from major bookstores, Amazon.com and bn.com.
Distributors include Ingram, Baker & Taylor and Bertram Books (UK).*

For more titles, new releases, and information visit our website at:
http://rockpublishing.com

CPSIA information can be obtained at www.ICGtesting.com
Printed in the USA
LVOW11s0508031113

359764LV00002B/607/A